SADIE'S STAR

COLLEEN MARIE

To Bill, my best friend and love
I am forever grateful to share this life with you.

CHAPTER ONE

A flash of lightning illuminates the night sky, casting an eerie glow on the murky road ahead. Heavy raindrops slam against the windshield as the glare from the headlights weave into misty swirls. My fingers curl tighter around the wheel in response to the abrupt bumps along the road. Perhaps what I'm driving on though shouldn't be called a road but more like a flooded dirt path to the unknown.

A scream rings out as another flash of lightning strikes nearby, sending a rippling jolt through my body

"What's happening?" Mom mumbles.

How she slept this long is beyond me. It's not the first time I've screamed during this storm. Straining to see the shaking navigator on the dashboard, she pulls herself upright on the seat.

"Here, let me drive. You need a break." She runs a hand through her short, tangled blonde hair and squints into the darkness.

I needed a break hours ago, but we're almost there now. I want to see it to the end. This is my journey, and I need to finish it. It wasn't really an offer anyway, and we both know it.

"I've got it. Just keep an eye out for the turn. It doesn't look like anyone around here thinks signs are important," I grumble.

Rippling with tension, I roll my head from side to side to loosen my neck and shoulder muscles. The muscles cling together in a desperate attempt to survive. I really can't blame them, so I focus on my breathing instead. The months of counseling taught me to observe my chest rising and falling with measured control. *One, two, three...*

Thunder rumbles across the sky, and I catch the navigator before it falls with its blinking screen alerting us of the upcoming road. Squinting to see anything in the dense, wooded darkness, I slow to a near crawl. Another bolt of lightning flashes, illuminating a faded green street sign.

Redwood Lane.

It stands out like a beacon navigating a lost ship. Gently steering down the lane, I notice my heartbeat finally begin to steady itself. The irregular beats regain their rhythm, and my thoughts wander once more into the darkness.

It was raining that day too. Big drops drenched the ground, and my clothing clung to my body as I ran as fast as I could. Beads of sweat settled on my chilled skin and goosebumps prickled the hairs of my neck. The fear and panic were suffocating as my lungs battled for air. It feels like years ago and yesterday all at once. No longer does the memory send me into a spiral of nerves but rather to a deadened state where everything feels numb.

I jump at the blaring horn of the truck behind us. Through the fading memory I see the familiar worry lines creased on Mom's face.

I press the accelerator. A dense darkness settles around us. The moon and stars hide behind the rumbling clouds. They're lucky. If only I could hide within the darkness too.

But if I did, would I ever be able to see light again?

THE RAINDROPS SLOW to a soft drizzle as we finally pull into the muddy driveway. The only sign of life is a faint light shining through the half-moon window of the rustic log cabin. Dark brown wood logs alternate with logs a shade lighter, giving it a smooth and dimensional appearance. A large front porch wraps around the sides to the back, hidden in the darkness. Two large flower beds filled with weeds flank the sides of the stone walkway.

"We're home," Mom says, holding the silver key up like a trophy.

This is our new home. "A new life," Mom promised. It's hard to think of this place as home since I've only ever lived in one place my whole life. And that place was my whole life. It was where I belonged until... I didn't anymore.

The light beckons us in, but it's hard to find the strength to get out of the Jeep. We saw pictures of the cabin before coming here but seeing it in person feels so different—familiar yet detached, like an empty, filtered photo from a social media page.

When Mom accepted the new veterinarian position at the Redwood Hills Biological Research Station, I thought it was a way to get me away from everything. The timing seemed almost too perfect. And then when they offered her this cabin to live in, everything was settled within a day. She never asked me if I wanted to leave, but just started packing our things in boxes.

"We're going to start a new life in Redwood Hills, California," she said that evening, with an unconvincing smile wobbling on her face. I quietly taped the boxes with displaced hostility as a single question reverberated in my mind: How could California ever be better than our home in Great Bear?

I grew up on a biological research base in the Great Bear Rainforest in British Columbia, where the green trees seemed endless, and the bubbling streams were the soundtrack to my life. Why would anyone want to leave?

I remind myself that we did leave. The memories made it unbearable to stay.

"Come on!" Mom calls, bringing me back to the present.

She wiggles the key in the lock before the door slowly creaks open. A large brass chandelier hangs from the ceiling, emitting the golden glow we saw from the Jeep. There is an openness I didn't expect from the photos. The planked ceiling arches toward the center, highlighting a twisted staircase. A skylight above the curved stairway allows moonlight to shine down into the living room. A quick glance is all I need to know that the stars will be visible on a clear night.

"So glad I had our furniture moved in ahead of time. It already feels like home." Mom looks around in awe. "Sadie, it's just perfect."

I wouldn't call our faded brown leather couch perfect, but it is a welcome sight after the long drive. The quilted throw pillows aren't scattered from one of mom's recent naps. The cushions are equally spaced on the couch with a precise organization that never existed before. I run my fingers along the familiar patchwork of each pillow and give each a tug, so they relax their stance. I remember carefully picking the color designs and stitching the pillow fabrics one piece at a time. I hold the pillow patterned with dark red, purple, and green. Corduroy is one of the tougher materials to sew, and I almost gave up but loved the texture too much. I'm glad I stuck it out.

The cream area rug is still as worn as ever, but now it lies in front of the most intricate stone fireplace I've ever seen. Its faded stones reach all the way to the arched ceiling. The stones are molded together in much the same way as the pillows, each one connected to the other, building a foundation for something lasting. I imagine someone building it, stone by stone, with each stone serving its own purpose. The precision and care it must have taken to build is evident in each stone's placement. The smoothness surprises me as I slide my hand over them like I used to with the river rocks at home.

"Isn't this cabin adorable, Sadie? Look at the cathedral ceiling and the crown molding..." Mom's voice breaks into my thoughts, but something else grabs my attention.

Our boxes lay waiting for us in the corner. We don't have many belongings, but what we couldn't fit into the Jeep, we sent ahead with the furniture. It looks like they survived the trip. Maybe there's still hope for us too.

"I'M GOING TO BED," I say about an hour later. My eyes are heavy from the day. "I'll finish tomorrow."

"Sure, goodnight love." Mom kisses my cheek before delving back into the boxes. At least her nap during the drive helped someone.

I carry one of my remaining boxes up the wooden stairs to my loft bedroom. Each step creaks in its unique melody under the pressure. I remember the layout from the photos and make my way easily into the loft while Mom continues to move about downstairs.

I stop for a moment and take in the room before me. Slanted edges run from the ceiling to the center of the soft white walls, creating a cozy nook. The walls are like a blank canvas, and I envision varying shades of green, yellow, and red mingling on each partition.

Two large open windows are centered on the back wall, looking out into the surrounding woods. Their pine shutters are unlatched, allowing a crisp breeze to flow through the room. The fresh, natural scent of rain and dirt is familiar and comforting. A drop of water falls from the window to a growing puddle on the hardwood floor—a reminder of the storm that just passed.

I turn to the sound of rustling papers and see my cedar loft bed sitting against the wall, the angled ceiling hugging it on each side. A perfect fit. My matching writing desk is tucked comfortably underneath. A small stack of papers sits on the cedar desktop with a note card next to it. The handmade card is crafted from a heavy and weathered cream paper with delicately embedded yellow flower petals and strands of grass. I open the card to reveal a short message written in small, neat script.

Sadie,

    Welcome to Redwood Hills! There is no better place to call home. I hope you and your mom feel comfortable with the cabin set up. I'm looking forward to getting to know you. We are all family here!

    Warmest regards,

    Ms. Maggie

No better place to call home. I used to feel that way about a very different place, but now there is no home for me anymore.

Placing the card back on the desk, I find myself gazing out the small window on the side wall. It's enclosed in a built-in window seat with a top hatch shutter in the same shade of redwood as the paneling. A small rope hooks to a brass latch on the ceiling. A deep golden yellow cushion covers the seat, with a few down feathers poking out of the canvas fabric. The window is open like the others, but there's no water. It's like a sanctuary in the storm.

I glance through the window and spot a soft light flickering through a clump of bent, twisted trees. I can make out the silhouette of another cabin, slightly larger than ours. Smoke billows out of the chimney in spiraling clouds. The light turns off as abruptly as it had come on, and the darkness blankets the trees again. I reach for the shutter latch but decide to leave it open instead. Somehow the fleeting light is a comfort.

I spot my small vanity wedged into the corner nook. Its oval mirror reflects a girl that I don't recognize anymore. A wave of sickness turns my stomach at the foreign image, and I walk to the center windows for a breath of fresh air. Inhaling the heavy air in gulps, I glimpse the starry sky. The clouds have cleared, and the sky is sparkling with millions of twinkling lights. I close my eyes for a moment, and the sound of the woods comes alive. Bugs chant, and leaves rustle a melody, as a wolf howls in the distance. It's a soundtrack that I have fallen asleep to my whole life. I press my forehead to the cold glass of the upper window.

Goosebumps prickle my skin, and a cold shiver runs down my spine. My eyes fly open as a dark shadow emerges from the trees. Its human form turns toward me, and my breath catches as I feel its eyes on me. The shape shifts slightly, sending a flash of light into the darkness, like a warning sent straight to me. My heart pounds, and my fight-or-flight instinct kicks in. But this time I don't have the urge to run like I normally do. Instead, I look directly at the shadowed figure for a long moment before it turns and disappears into the woods.

I turn away from the window and flick the light off. The darkness sheltering me from the stranger. Could he be a neighbor? Maybe checking the land for storm damage?

I close the windows and secure the shutters. Left with a nauseating uneasiness, I climb up onto my bed and curl into a ball under my worn patchwork quilt. The heavy fabric embraces me. Unwilling to open my eyes, I feel myself drifting away.

My feet sink into the mud of the riverbank. There's freedom in the gentle breeze and warmth of the sun's light streaming through the trees. I dip my bare feet in the chilly water and breathe in the musty scent of the forest, allowing it to nourish the emptiness within me. Sticks snap as a white bear pushes through the brush. The sunlight fades suddenly as a somber cloud covers the sky, and a darkness descends into my bones. I catch the bear's eye. There's sadness swirling in the caramel depths. A heavy foreboding overwhelms me. I reach for her, but she is gone.

I awaken damp with sweat. The brightness of the loft assaults my eyes and dots flash like fireworks as my eyes adjust.

I take a deep breath. It was just a dream.

But it felt so real. It was like I was in Great Bear on my favorite riverbank with Angel. My heart squeezes at the thought of my favorite spirit bear.

I need air.

My muscles ache as I climb down the ladder of my bunk. I push the side window all the way up and pause at the sound of the flapping wings of a small bird. As the cool air flows over me, I study the bird as it swoops away and then returns with a few twigs in its thin beak. The beginning of a nest is visible in the alcove at the base of the roof.

A cloud shifts. Sunlight streams through the window and reflects off the buckle of my clothing chest. The chest traveled with the furniture, and it feels like a lifetime ago that I packed it—not the mere week it has been. I run my finger over the clasp. Opening the chest is opening up my past.

I groan. As much as I would like to put it off or ignore it, I need to shower and get dressed. I'd rather stay here and take my time unpacking, but Mom asked me to go the clinic with her this morning. And, of course, I promised her that I would. Sometimes I wish there was just one day when I could think only of myself and not worry about what's best for everyone else.

I know today is not that day though. So, whether I'm ready or not, it's time. I take another deep breath and push any remaining thoughts of the dream into the back of my mind. I sit next to the chest and slowly lift the lid. A lump forms in my throat. It smells like Great Bear. It's as if I packed a capsule of air with my clothing because I knew I would need it when I arrived. The familiar slightly mossy scent with just a tint of firewood drifts around me. I inhale deeply, savoring the moment before it's gone forever.

When I finally open my eyes, dampness threatens my lashes from unshed tears. I take in the collection of dresses lying just as I packed them. I lift the sleeveless white cotton dress from the trunk and run my thumb over the peach roses embroidered around the neckline. The softness feels like home in my hands. I designed it for those carefree summer days—days I fear are only in the past now.

"A white dress won't last long in the forest," Dad said once with a shake of his head. But I didn't care what anyone thought. From the very first moment I saw the fabric at the market, I knew exactly what kind of dress I would make. Each of my dresses has a purpose and reason for the design. Each fits a different part of me, and it's been a long time since I've worn this white dress. The dress represents a part of me that I'm not sure exists anymore.

I hold it up to the sunlight streaming from the open window. It begins to flutter in the breeze. The thin, white cotton swirls around and around until my thoughts are no longer in my loft but back in a place I long for desperately.

"Sadie? It's time for breakfast." Mom's voice rings out, and the stairs creek with each approaching step.

I jump up before Mom can reach the door. "I'll be down in a minute," I snap.

The stairs are silent for a moment before the creaking resumes as she descends. When her footsteps subside, I hurry downstairs into the hallway bathroom.

"We need to leave soon. Take a quick one, okay?" Mom calls to me above the clinking of dishes in the kitchen. "Oh, and there are towels in the cabinet next to the sink."

I yank a fluffy, white towel from the bathroom cabinet and throw it onto the hook by the shower. An oval-shaped window sits next to it, revealing a clear view out into the woods. Closing the blinds with a flick of the cord, I step into the marble-walled shower and turn the water as hot as I can stand. Allowing the hot water to run over me and loosen my muscles, I hope to erase the dream from my mind.

JUST BEFORE NINE, we pull into the long gravel driveway of the research center. I twist the last strands of my damp hair into a braid, letting it fall over my shoulder. I barely had enough time after showering to do anything other than to slip on the white sundress and lace up my brown leather hiking boots. When Mom parks the Jeep, I look up and see another log cabin. This one is larger and newer than ours. It blends in with the surrounding trees, like an extension of the forest itself.

A large, white oval sign hangs from the top of the entrance. A twisted rope secures the heavy wood etched in green with a single redwood tree and the words "Redwood Hills Research Center" carved boldly across. Opening the heavy wooden door, we walk into the front lobby as an earthy aroma of mild spice with sweet undertones envelopes us. Wood beams line the ceiling, offering not just strength but a rustic charm.

"Good morning! And how can I help you beautiful ladies this morning?" A woman peeks out from behind a large desk and greets us with a wide grin edged in bright red lipstick. Looking to be in her seventies with short white hair and a plump, round face, she has an unusual energy about her.

"Good morning," Mom replies cheerfully. "I'm Dr. Samantha Foster. I'm here to meet with Dr. Allen."

The woman's eyes light with recognition. "Why yes, of course!" A mischievous glint flashes in her eyes. "Well, it is a pleasure to finally meet you. I'm Maggie Cole, the always-reliable receptionist and well, main lady around here. If you need anything—anything at all—all you have to do is ask."

Ms. Maggie smiles so big that smears of red lipstick mark her teeth, creating a somewhat frenzied and feral appearance. Mom looks at Ms. Maggie like she just discovered a new species, while Ms. Maggie continues to smile back at her. I can almost see Mom's mind trying to categorize her into a genus and species, while mentally recording her characteristics. It's an odd feeling to find myself having to hold in my laughter. I can't remember the last time I laughed out loud.

"Well, thank you Ms. Maggie," Mom finally says. "I do appreciate that, and it is so nice to meet you too. If you could point me in the direction of Dr. Allen that would be wonderful."

"By golly, I'll do more than that. I'll take you to him myself."

She walks around the desk, limping slightly as she moves. She's wearing the khaki uniform of the park rangers.

"I've been here so long, they've gone ahead and given me my own uniform," she says, winking at me. "This right leg of mine is a bit down for the count though. But no worries about that! No mountain lion is going to take a bite out of me without good ol' Ms. Maggie fighting back."

Mom's mouth hangs agape while I take a step closer to Ms. Maggie.

Ms. Maggie is clearly enjoying every moment. "Oh, don't worry your pretty little heads over this! That mountain lion was going after my darling Fluffy, and nobody messes with my baby. I always protect my own." She points a manicured finger at us.

"Fluffy?" Mom raises an eyebrow.

"Oh, she's the cutest thing! Let Mama show you a picture or two." Ms. Maggie takes Mom's hand and pulls her back around to her desk, showing her the six framed photos of her little Yorkshire terrier.

"She's adorable," I say. "Especially dressed up as a cowgirl."

"Is this from Halloween?" Mom asks while analyzing the cowgirl photo.

I swear she looks like she's about to start a new field journal on poor Ms. Maggie. I feel a tug of pity for Ms. Maggie, but that may be unnecessary as she can clearly take care of herself.

"What? No, why would you think that? That's her county fair outfit. She is quite the looker at the fair! Everyone says so. Funny you picked out that photo though. It was not long after the fair when that lion came for her. Jealous if you ask me—jealousy is the root of all evil," she says with experience evident in her tone. "We were sitting out having ourselves some afternoon tea that very next day, and I was throwing her little ball for her, like she loves so much, when out of nowhere the mountain lion came darting out of the woods and straight for my Fluffy! I jumped from my seat, running as fast as I could. My little darling was barking and growling at that monstrous cat. Such a brave little girl she is. I got there just in time to stop the beast, but not before she had one good swipe at my ol' leg here."

I find that I'm beginning to really like Ms. Maggie.

"Oh, Colin could hardly believe that I fought that lion and won. I told him I have fight in me. He still comes by and checks on me every day. He's a catch that one."

"Colin?" I ask.

"Why yes, darling, Colin. He's the park ranger. Ranger Anderson. Best park ranger we've ever had. And handsome too." Ms. Maggie shoots a pointed look at Mom.

Mom begins to twist the gold wedding band around her finger. I look away, unable to watch the sadness flood her eyes and notice a stack of stationary paper on Ms. Maggie's desk. Handmade pressed flowers and grass.

"You're the one who set up our cabin."

Ms. Maggie nods and clears her throat. "Why, yes dear. I hope you ladies like it. And if you need help with anything, just let me know. Ranger Anderson and Ronan moved all of the furniture. I just made it a bit...homier."

"Thank you," Mom gushes. "That was so kind of you all. It really is a lovely cabin.

"Yeah, thanks," I say, "and for the note too. You're stationary is amazing."

Ms. Maggie studies me for a moment. "So glad you like it. Every girl deserves a nice stationary set."

Mom flashes me a questioning look, but I quickly turn away.

"Well now, why don't I take you to see Dr. Allen. And you," Ms. Maggie says, sending me another wink, "can pick any seat you'd like. I'll be back before the raccoons come to town."

They leave through a side door as Ms. Maggie tells a story about raccoons, encouraging Mom's laughter. Choosing the most inconspicuous seat against the back wall, I slouch down behind the large, green fern towering beside it.

Finally, alone. I don't know if Redwood Hills could ever be home, but this place could be more interesting than I thought.

I explore the lobby as I wait for Ms. Maggie to return. Pausing in front of the large corner bookcase, I scan the textbooks, novels, and magazines. There is a variety of science textbooks, wildlife reference books, and literary journals. Among these are both classic and contemporary novels, ranging from John Steinbeck to John Green. Sticking out from between the books are picture books, crossword puzzles and sudoku, and even a coloring book with a box of used crayons. I would normally be surprised by the range of topics and haphazard arrangement, but after meeting Ms. Maggie, I just give a little smile and shake my head. I get the distinct feeling she organized this bookcase.

As I reach for the new edition of *National Geographic*, boots sound on the front steps. I quickly scoot back to my seat and try to blend in behind the potted fern. I pull out the small notebook from my bag and begin sketching. The moment the pencil hits the paper, my nerves begin to settle.

The door opens, and a large man walks into the lobby followed by a teenage boy. The boy looks to be about sixteen, like me. I immediately lower my eyes and hope they don't notice me.

"Wonder where Ms. Maggie could've gone," the boy says. He's close to six-feet tall with a lean, but muscular build. A San Francisco Giants baseball hat shades his profile.

"Who could say?" the man asks, with a dismissive shake of his head. "You know Ms. Maggie."

The boy grunts in agreement and pauses at the same *National Geographic* I was eyeing. After rolling it up, he sticks it into his back pocket. Great, so much for learning about the California sea lions. And who rolls up new magazines like that and then sticks them in their pockets?

"I wonder if the new vet is in yet," the man says as he stares out of the window. "If she's anything like that crooked McFadden, we're goin' to have some trouble."

"Can't imagine the new vet would be so awful, but it doesn't hurt to be careful. I'm sure Detective Miller is keeping an eye on him," the boy says as he joins him at the window.

Wait, what happened with the last vet? Whatever it was must have led to the open position Mom filled.

"Yeah, we'll see. I'll tell you one thing: I won't let another vet turn on us the way he did," the man grunts. "Alright, let's unload the wood first and then stop back in to see Ms. Maggie."

Through the feathery fronds of the fern, the boy catches my eye. Surprise crosses his face and then something else.

Interest?

My cheeks begin to burn as he gives me a slight nod before following the man out the door. I release a deep sigh.

Who is he?

Curiosity gets the better of me and I walk over to the window, glancing out of the corner. They're moving logs from the back of a white Dodge Ram pick-up truck and building a pile on the side of the lodge. The boy must feel my stares because he catches my eye again and this time he sends me a slight smile. The action catches me off guard, and I immediately turn away and hurry back to my seat and open my notebook. With his smile still in my mind, I pick up my pencil and begin drawing. My heart thumps in a way it never has before. When I glance down, the page reflects the face of the boy, and his eyes look right into mine.

CHAPTER TWO

A little while later, Ms. Maggie returns to the main lobby. She sits in her desk chair and rocks back and forth with a thoughtful look on her face.

"Is my mom coming back?" I ask.

Ms. Maggie startles. "Oh, dear," she gasps, putting a hand over her heart. "I didn't even see you back there. That plant is bigger than you!" She peers at me, like she's seeing me for the first time. "Your mom is catching up with Dr. Allen. Why don't you go into the break room and get yourself a donut." She points to the small room to my left.

I want to stay and ask her about the previous vet, but my stomach growls, reminding me that I haven't eaten yet. "Okay, sounds good," I say, slipping my notebook and pencil back into my leather bag.

Slinging the bag over my shoulder, I go into the break room and see a huge assortment of donuts from a local bakery. The brown boxes are open, revealing Boston cream, chocolate frosted, cinnamon pecan, peach cobbler, and more. I'm about to pick a caramel-glazed donut when I hear the front door open again and the sound of work boots coming into the lobby.

"Colin and Ronan! I've been waiting for you two. The new vet is here," Ms. Maggie exclaims, with what could only be described as a crazed glee in her voice.

So, that was Ranger Anderson. And apparently the mysterious magazine roller is Ronan. I close the breakroom door to just a crack to have a clear view of the main desk and lobby. I catch Ronan glancing in the direction of the fern, causing a warm flush to creep up my neck.

"She's here?" Ranger Anderson asks.

"She sure is." Ms. Maggie nods to Mom and another man as they walk into the lobby from the side door.

Ranger Anderson stares unabashedly at my mom. It's almost comical. But to be fair this isn't really surprising since my mom is strikingly beautiful with her smooth alabaster skin, large green eyes, and short, curly blond hair.

"Colin, I'd like you to meet Dr. Samantha Foster, our new vet." Ms. Maggie looks pointedly at him, as if trying to mentally send him a message.

Ranger Anderson's jaw drops, and Mom gives him a questioning look. When Ranger Anderson doesn't say anything, Ms. Maggie continues with the introductions.

"Dr. Foster—this is Ranger Colin Anderson, and his assistant ranger, Ronan O'Connor. Let me tell you, you'll never find men like these two anywhere else than right here in Redwood Hills."

Ranger Anderson finally regains his composure and shakes Mom's hand, holding it longer than normal. Mom turns to greet Ronan as Ranger Anderson continues to watch her, hands in his pockets. Ronan gives Mom a smile.

Ranger Anderson mumbles something about needing to get back to work, but not before giving Mom one last unnerving stare and a curt nod to the tall, slender man standing next to her. There's an awkward silence in the lobby after they leave. Ms. Maggie doesn't seem a bit perturbed though. She continues to smile as though it's the best day in the world.

I grab a Boston cream donut for Mom before joining them in the lobby. Mom's confident smile is back as she takes a small bite of the donut. She's always so strong when she's working. It's when it's just us that her stability begins to crumble.

"Sadie, I'd like you to meet Dr. Eric Allen."

I turn to the man next to her for the first time. His dark, unnerving eyes are intent on mine as he shakes my hand. His hand is too warm and his grip too hard. I try to pull my hand away, but he holds it a moment longer before finally releasing me.

I need fresh air.

"Let's go for a tour of the research center," Mom suggests.

The three of us walk outside into the crisp mountain air, and I finally feel like I can breathe again.

I WATCH as Dr. Allen and Mom laugh together on our way to the research center. Why am I only now learning that they were such good friends during their undergrad days at Berkeley? There's a comfort between them that reveals a history I don't understand.

"I didn't realize you guys were such great friends," I say, breaking into their conversation.

Mom begins chewing her bottom lip and looks into the woods.

Dr. Allen flashes me a smile. "We were lab partners since freshman year. Your mother was one of the best at dissections. Something to be proud of in our department."

He winks at mom, and my stomach turns.

"I guess that's good to know since she's a vet and all. The animals appreciate that."

"Sadie, watch your tone," Mom warns.

Dr. Allen glances between us. "I have no doubt that she's the best vet around. After graduation, when your mom went to Washington State for veterinary school, I knew she'd do very well. I, on the other hand, stayed behind at Berkeley for graduate school." His mouth forms a tight line. "A research position within the biology department," he adds.

"So, it sounds like you've kept in touch over the years." I shoot Mom a pointed look.

Dr. Allen's smile is back. "Now and again."

We walk through a sliding glass door and into a shiny, white hallway. The hardwood floor is spotless, and the walls are blank except for a laboratory safety poster. "And you're the one that offered Mom the position here?" I ask.

"I sure am. When our last vet didn't work out, your mom was the first person that came to mind. We're lucky to have her expertise here."

Seeing them together, I can feel a history there and can't help but wonder why I had never heard of Dr. Allen before a few weeks ago. There's something different about him than the other scientists Mom has worked with. His intense focus is like a sea wolf tracking its prey.

"So, Sadie," Mom says clearing her throat, "the research station is incredible, isn't it? It's a lot like the one at Great Bear, just a bit larger and with newer equipment."

Dr. Allen laughs a knowing laugh as if this is an inside joke between the two of them and it makes my skin crawl. A sense of protectiveness washes over me as I think about our old home.

Great Bear's research center is a small, three-room structure next to the base. There is a presentation and meeting room, a work room with animal specimens, and a laboratory. The meeting room can hold about ten to fifteen people if everyone sits very close together, but the lab can only hold four people, and the work room is better with just one or two people in addition to the cages and storage cabinets. But it's welcoming and comfortable in the design details with its warm gold walls and deep red accents. There are even a couple of handmade quilts with animal prints I helped to sew in the blocks—a stark contrast to the bright white walls of the Redwood research station and shiny new instruments and gadgets. Here it feels like a brand-new house that's being staged—one that doesn't have the welcoming touch of a family.

Mom nudges me. "Sadie, are you listening?"

I nod and try my best to look normal and not like I was replaying the same memories over again in my mind, which, of course, I was.

"Yeah. It's great." I pretend to look interested. I know it was the right thing to say because I see a big smile spread on Mom's face. She doesn't seem to notice my superficial response or the strain in my voice. But it's always easier when I don't let my emotions show. I guess that doesn't change whether I'm here or back in Great Bear.

"It really is incredible. See, the clinic is right next to the main center." We walk out another set of sliding glass doors, and she points to the small log cabin clinic adjacent to the clinic.

As we walk through the front door, I notice a warm glow from the dozen rustic wall lanterns. A variety of animal photos hang on the deep blue walls. They are vibrant and display dogs, cats, and wild animals. There's one photo of an adorable dark-haired boy, maybe five or six years old, hugging his large brown dog. The dog's front leg is bandaged, and the boy's expression holds not just pleasure but pride. Another photo shows a teenage girl with short, pink hair holding a spotted skunk. The black and white fur and inquisitive look is an interesting combination. The girl is mid-laugh as the fluffy tail tickles her cheek.

"There are so many resources that I've never had before," Mom says, breaking my attention. "The operating room is state-of-the-art— really innovative. And over there, just to the right of the clinic, is the Redwood Hills Animal Sanctuary."

Now that catches my attention. I look through the open side window at the large enclosure that stretches so far back that I can't see the end. Just like the main research center and the clinic, the animal sanctuary lodge is a log cabin with a green shingled roof that seems to blend in with the surroundings.

The howl of a wolf fills the air, but the tone isn't like the coastal wolves I'm used to in British Columbia. I'm about to ask about the type of wolf it is when Dr. Allen turns to me, causing the question to get caught in my throat.

"So, your mom tells me you have a love for animals and a very special connection with them."

I wonder how much she told him about me when she's barely spoken a word about him?

I nod, forcing myself to look at him. A flash of light catches my eye. A large silver pin on his vest reflects the sunlight as he turns to me once more. A symbol is etched into it, but it's hard to see the exact detail from my distance.

"So," he says, bringing my attention back to him, "I was thinking you may like to work at the sanctuary. We are looking for another research technician, and it sounds like you would be perfect for the role. It would mostly be observing and recording animal behavior. We're looking to compile a database of behaviors to benefit our current research. There would be other duties as well, such as some cleaning and feeding, but overall, it would be basically an internship in animal behavior. Not so bad for the résumé." He winks at me. "What do you think?"

Out of the corner of my eye, I see a bald eagle swooping through the nearby trees and for the first time in Redwood Hills, a peace settles over me.

"How soon can I start?"

<hr>

AFTER A QUICK TOUR of the exam rooms, I've had enough of the scent of rubbing alcohol and shiny instruments.

"I'm going to take a walk," I tell Mom as she pulls on a pair of chemical splash goggles.

"That's a great idea. Enjoy this weather. The sun feels so good today."

She gives me a quick kiss on the cheek before I walk down the long hallway and out the double wooden doors.

The sun is bright and there's a faint scent of wildflowers in the air. I don't know how people can work inside for any length of time. It always feels like the walls are closing in on me. I'm used to being outside. While I spent some time inside the research base at Great Bear, it was never for long. I was always out exploring the forest. I would usually hike with my parents or the research team, and while they were collecting data, I would climb up the red cedar trees and look for mountain goats or Sitka deer. Once I climbed high enough to see a grizzly bear in the distance. I never felt scared when I was with the research team. While I didn't understand all the equipment, I knew they were prepared for anything.

It was on one of those walks when I first encountered a spirit bear. I was following the team back to the base when I slipped away from them to explore a trail leading to the river, and I saw the white bear. Spirit bears are a subspecies of the American black bear, but a genetic mutation makes their fur white or cream colored. Mom and Dad always told me how they are a unique and beautiful example of God's creation. They devoted their life to studying the bears. So it was only natural that from a young age, I had a special interest in them as well.

That day, her white fur stood out against the emerald green surroundings. She was rubbing her back against a tree, and I remember laughing out loud at the sight. I was only nine years old at the time, and my laughter was pure and free. She heard me, and her ears shot up as she looked my way. I was carefree and had no fear back then. She looked me right in the eye, and I knew with the innocence of a child that she would never harm me.

I strolled to the edge of the stream of water trickling over the tree roots and gazed at her. She looked right back at me, and the connection lit up her eyes. "We'll be friends forever," I told her.

If Mom and Dad had seen me, they would have been furious because they always taught me to respect a bear's space and to never go near them on my own. But in that moment, I was drawn to her. When I heard Mom calling for me a few minutes later, I walked back to the base. My new friend followed me the whole way. Mom's eyes grew large when she saw us coming.

"Sadie, don't make any sudden moves," she warned.

I laughed and turned to point at the bear. "She's Angel, my new friend."

"Angel?" The panic was rising in her voice.

"Yes, Angel. That's what I named her."

"Sadie, walk slowly through the gate, and shut it behind you. No sudden movements."

"Oh, Mom," I said, rolling my eyes. "Bye, Angel! I'll see you tomorrow!"

Giving the bear a wave, I walked right past Mom and into the base.

Lost in the memory, I find myself at the entrance of the animal sanctuary. I try the front door, but it's locked.

I sit on one of the Adirondack chairs on the large front porch, appreciating the cool morning breeze flowing around me. I soon notice a dirt trail leading to the woods. Without a second thought, I follow the path until I'm at the entrance to the woods. The memory of my nine-year-old adventurous heart, a heart that had not yet been injured, comes back to me. I take a few steps into the woods and feel more at home than I have since coming here. The canopy of trees envelops and comfort me. The sound of my boots hit the hard dirt path in unison to the beating of my heart.

I look up to the towering redwood trees, arching over me to create a canopy overhead. Large areas of moss and light grey mushrooms cover the damp ground. I step over them as best I can and reach out to feel the ferns lining the path. The fuzzy texture tickles my palm, and I laugh out loud. The sound echoes in the surrounding trees, and a group of wood warblers fly out of a nearby shrub. I stop to watch them fly in a single flock to a nearby shrub.

A branch breaks and stirs a chipmunk to dart across my boot. I freeze for a moment before the adrenaline kicks in. I take off and recall the last time I ran through the woods. Stumbling on a root, I tumble to the hard ground, twisting my ankle. Wincing from the pain, I stand but can't put my weight on the injured ankle. I try to hop with my good foot when a loud bark breaks my focus. A large animal jumps up and knocks me back to the ground. But instead of devouring me, he licks my face.

"Rocky, no!"

It's Ronan. This time he isn't wearing his hat, and his brown hair hangs over his forehead and frames his matching caramel brown eyes. I feel like the wind has been knocked out of me, but it's not from the dog. I stare at him as he pulls the chocolate lab off me. He attempts to get the dog to sit down, but Rocky is doing everything he can to get back to me.

I stand up and stumble. Ronan grabs hold of my arm to help steady me. His touch is gentle but strong. Rocky now sits at his side panting with what looks like utter joy and excitement. I push his hand away, trying to regain my control.

"You need to train that dog," I snap. My nerves are shaken. "What kind of idiot lets his dog run wild?" I know I'm taking my feelings out on him, but the words still come.

He narrows his eyes at me. "He is trained. Well, he's in training." Ronan shrugs. "Just a bit excitable, and it seems that he likes you. I thought he had good instincts."

His retort hurts even though I know it's somewhat deserved. When I give him my best sneer, he looks more confused than insulted.

"And 'hi' is a normal greeting when meeting someone, just so you know," he says with a look of confusion like he's struggling with a complex algebra problem.

"Well, I guess greetings aren't really my thing." It feels like my heart is building a wall with each word. Survival of the fittest, right?"

I try to maintain my defiant stance, but honestly, I just want to give him a big hug. The dog, not Ronan. Well, at least I think so.

"I guess politeness isn't really your thing either."

"Nope, I guess not."

We look at each other with a barely contained disgust. I know that I started this, and I want to stop. But if you get close to people, you can lose them. I know this all too well.

"Okay, well, sorry about Rocky. He didn't mean any harm. He's a good dog, just a little energetic." He looks at me with disappointment as he begins to walk away. Then he stops and turns back. "But you know—you shouldn't be out in the woods alone anyway. You're not from around here, and if you think you know what you're doing in these woods, you're wrong."

I may have felt bad about my behavior a moment ago, but his arrogance is infuriating. I don't know what I'm doing in the woods? He has no idea.

"I can handle myself just fine. I don't need an arrogant, self-righteous guy telling me what to do. And these woods are nothing compared to the ones I grew up in. So just leave me alone."

I stomp back through the woods. Pain shoots through my ankle with each step. I don't dare chance a look behind. Because if I did that, he would see the tears sliding down my cheeks.

CHAPTER THREE

I'm quiet as Mom drives to the local diner later that afternoon. The confrontation with Ronan weighs heavily on my mind.

"It's just incredible the number of resources at my disposal," Mom says, more to herself than me. "I mean technical equipment that I've only read about, right there in front of me. It's a dream."

A dream. A nightmare. There's a fine line between the two.

"Sounds like you're really happy."

"We can choose to be happy, Sadie. Even in the grief and sadness."

Funny how she says that now, but who always has to be strong when she falls apart? Me. I choose not to speak my thoughts and look out the window instead.

Gravel crunches under the tires as we pull into a crowded parking lot. A glance in the rearview mirror confirms what I expected. My hair is a mess. We drove with the top down, and my long, blonde hair broke free of the braid. Now it's as wild as I've ever seen it. I run my fingers through the loose curls and pull it back into a messy ponytail, untangling my golden feather earrings from the strands. I wipe the smudges of brown eyeliner from the corner of my green eyes.

"You'll have to put more ice on that ankle when we get home," Mom tells me.

My ankle has swollen a little, and there's a purple bruise developing on outer side. I barely feel it anymore though. I decide not to say any more about it, opting to change the subject instead.

"So, what's with all the log cabins?"

The diner is, of course, another rustic log cabin, which I'm finding to be the norm for this place.

Mom laughs. "Redwood Hills is the log-cabin capital of the Pacific Northwest, or at least that's what Ms. Maggie told me earlier. She's interesting, isn't she? There's something I can't put my finger on..." She gets a far-off look in her eyes that she always gets when she's trying to solve a puzzle.

"She's not a species to be studied," I remind her with a bit more attitude than I intend.

"Anyway," she says, without acknowledging my remark, "I love the cabins. They're so charming. Ms. Maggie said the community takes great pride in them, and most are family-built and maintained. There's a strong sense of unity and love of this land. I respect that. It's not so very different from Great Bear, Sadie."

Just the mention of our old home sends a wave of homesickness over me. I long to be back there, but at the same time, I can't imagine ever returning to our small bungalow. My bottom lip begins to quiver as tears sting my eyes once again.

"Let's get dinner," Mom says, hopping out of the Jeep.

I follow her into the diner. Avoiding emotions is the way we do things.

THE DINER BUSTLES with overpacked tables. It appears that the whole town comes here to eat. There's conversation and laughter ringing throughout. A girl with short dark hair and bright blue eyes greets us at the front door and leads us to a small table for two. She's giving me an odd look, not unfriendly, but like she's judging me in some way. She continues to watch us as our waitress comes to our table.

"Hello! My name is Gia, and I will be serving you today. Can I get you something to drink?"

Our waitress looks to be about my age. Her long black hair is tied into a ponytail high on the top of her head, and it swishes as she talks. Her eyes are edged in black eyeliner, and bright red lipstick coats her generous smile, creating a dramatic effect that's enhanced by the tiny diamond stud in her nose. She screams of creativity beneath her faded red diner apron.

"Hi Gia. I would love an iced tea," Mom chimes.

I ask for a water, and Gia smiles at me with a warmness I wasn't ready for. When she leaves, my mom leans in and whispers, "I think that's Eric's niece."

"Eric?"

"Yes, Dr. Allen," she whispers. "He was telling me how his niece came to live in Redwood last year. Apparently, she was getting into some trouble back in Maryland, and her parents thought a change would be good for her. Her older sister moved to Redwood a few years ago after she married and offered to take Gia in. Dr. Allen is helping to keep an eye on her too. He said she's doing great here. Sometimes you just need a fresh start." She gives me a meaningful look, and I look away, biting my tongue.

Mom nudges me. "She's going to be a junior this year, just like you. Maybe she can help show you around the school."

I was homeschooled on the base in Great Bear, and except for a few trips to Vancouver every year, it has always just been the families on the base. It was more like our schooling was a part of life and not a separate aspect of the day. We learned throughout the day in our daily activities. Sitting in a classroom will be very different from the family room or outdoor picnic area where we spent most of our lesson time.

"Maybe," I reply.

"Thank you, dear." Mom grins at Gia, who places our drinks on the table. "What would you recommend? We are new in town. My daughter, Sadie, will be joining Redwood Academy this fall."

Subtle Mom.

"Oh, that's great." Gia smiles. "I moved here last year and just love it. Only two weeks of summer left before school, and I'm trying to enjoy every moment, you know?"

We laugh but as I have never attended a physical school, I don't really know or understand at all.

"As for food recommendations," Gia continues, "I recommend the chicken pot pie. It's my favorite. And an ice cream sundae afterward. They're super good!"

We take her advice, which does not disappoint. The chicken pot pies are the best we've ever had, and we order ice cream sundaes for dessert. Mom chooses her normal chocolate ice cream, whipped cream, and rainbow sprinkles. I order vanilla ice cream with whipped cream, waffle pieces, and three cherries—because one isn't enough, and four is too many.

"And here are your sundaes!" Gia puts three sundaes on the table. "Mind if I join you? It's my break, and I can't pass up ice cream."

We nod, and she slides into a chair and lifts her spoon like it's a momentous occasion. "Time to dig in!"

Sharing this time with Gia reminds me of Anna, my best friend at Great Bear. She's one of eight children of the legendary Dr. Jay Whitefield, the Coastal First Nations lead naturalist on the research base. I called him Papa Jay when I was little, and the name stuck over the years. Papa Jay was like another father to me and my mentor. He encouraged me in my studies and introduced me to many native species in Great Bear. Mom and Dad were often involved in their own research and work, so Papa Jay would teach many of the science courses to me, Anna, and the other children from the local indigenous community. As a child I was in awe of him, but as I grew older, my awe turned into more of a deeply rooted respect and love. The fact that he looked out for me like another daughter only strengthened my relationship with Anna.

People used to call us sisters because we were inseparable growing up on the base. Without any brothers or sisters of my own, she really was like my sister. We did our homeschool classes together, studying together and quizzing each other on topics from the American Revolution to photosynthesis to Jane Austen. To leave her and the Whitefield family was like leaving my childhood and family behind in one move. Anna and I promised to keep in touch and save money so she could visit, but she seems so far away now. Another wave of homesickness begins to build, but I push it back down, straightening my back.

Taking my first spoonful of ice cream, I let out an exaggerated groan. "This is so good."

"Told you!" Gia leans closer to Mom to read the badge on her shirt. "Oh, you're Dr. Foster. I just realized. My uncle works at the research station, and he was talking about a new vet coming to the clinic. You're all he has been talking about actually. He's really excited you're joining their team."

Is it just me or did the entire diner get quiet? The man in the red-and-black flannel shirt holds his fork of barbeque pork inches from his mouth but doesn't take a bite while the lady across from him slowing stirs her lemonade, head tilted our way. Gia doesn't seem fazed though.

"That's so sweet." Mom smiles. "I just started today, but I can already tell it's going to be a great fit."

"You're brave," Gia says, shaking her head. "After what happened with Dr. McFadden, I don't think the town can take anymore drama. What a mess that was. Nearly ruined the town and was the talk for months."

"What happened?" I ask.

Gia glances around the diner. "Well, I can't get into it all here, but he was arrested for involvement in a poaching ring."

"What kind of poaching?"

"No one knows. Or if they do, they're not saying."

I glance at Mom and notice a crease between her brows. This is news to her as well. The team at Great Bear always warned of potential poaching, especially with a rare animal like the spirit bears. As a community, we spent a lot of time making sure the environment was safe for the bears and other wildlife.

Gia slides back into her seat. "Uncle Eric spends most of his time at the research base. I keep telling him he needs more fun in his life, but he just says how much he loves his work." She takes one last scoop of her chocolate ice cream and sighs.

"Although," she whispers, "I think if he hadn't been so in love with his work Aunt Cila and Jonathon wouldn't have left him."

"Your uncle was married?" Mom asks with surprise. "We were

friends from university. We kept in touch over the years, but he never mentioned he was married."

If they were such good friends, how could she not have known that he was married? The questions are piling up.

"Yeah, they separated about three years ago now. Right after little Jonathon was born. One day, she just left with Jonathon and moved to San Diego. As far as I know Uncle Eric doesn't talk to them much at all."

"I'm so sorry to hear that." Mom shifts in her seat.

Gia nods before finishing her sundae and then sighs. "You reap what you sow, as my sister always says."

"Sadly so," Mom agrees.

Gia turns to me. "Sadie, have you met Ronan yet? He works at the research station too. At the sanctuary actually."

My heart trips at the mention of Ronan.

"O-Oh, yeah," I stammer. "I met him today. His dog too."

Mom's attention perks up at this.

"Rocky! Love that dog. He's adorable, isn't he?" Gia giggles so loudly that I glance around the diner feeling a bit self-conscious. But as I glance around, everyone seems engaged in conversation again— except for one. The dark-haired hostess stares directly at us.

Mom gently nudges me with her foot.

"Yeah, he's cute." An image of Ronan flashes through my mind. "Wait, Rocky or Ronan?" My face immediately begins to burn with embarrassment.

"Both, right?" Gia laughs. "I meant Rocky, but Ronan is a cutie too. And he's such a great guy. Plays baseball for school, and he's really good. Everyone says he's going to get a scholarship for it."

I don't know how to respond, so I remain silent. And clearly, I can't trust what I say right now.

"Well," Gia says, standing and stretching her arms over her head, "my break is over. Thanks for letting me hang out with you guys."

I can feel Mom ready to start in with the questions, and I suddenly wish I was the one in the waitress uniform with a reason to get up and leave. I know she wants to ask me about Ronan, but thankfully Gia returns with the check.

"Sadie, if you're not busy Friday, there's an outdoor movie night at the school. It should be fun. I can introduce you to some people from school." Gia smiles at me.

Mom nudges me, but I stay quiet.

"She would love that! Sadie, how nice."

"Sure, thanks." The words finally come out. "That sounds fun."

"Great! Here's my cell." She writes her number on a napkin. "We're not allowed to have our phones on us during work." She rolls her eyes. "Just text me, and we'll meet up. The movie starts at eight—and bring a blanket!"

As we leave the diner, I wonder if I could ever fit in here. I'm still considering this when we return to the cabin. Mom parks the Jeep as a ping sounds on her phone.

After reading the text message, she looks at me. "Dr. Allen set up a meeting for you and the technician manager at the animal sanctuary. It's at nine tomorrow morning."

Despite the uneasiness residing in the pit of my stomach, this job really does sound like a dream, even if that means I owe Dr. Allen for it. Something about that just doesn't sit right.

I WAKE the next morning with the rising sun. My nervousness is turning to excitement as I think of the animals in the sanctuary. It's the one place since being here where I have felt any sense of peace—a peace that reminds me that there is hope for a new beginning and maybe even a chance to leave the past behind.

"How's your ankle today, Sadie darling?" Ms. Maggie asks as soon as we walk into the research center. I guess news really does travel quickly in a small town. The wide, purple bandana wrapped around her head is losing its battle with her wild hair. I can't imagine Ms. Maggie being tied down by anything.

"It's fine. Just like new," I tell her, which is mostly true. There's still a little swelling, but my hiking socks cover it well. Nothing is going to stop me from going to the sanctuary this morning.

"I'm so glad to hear it!" Ms. Maggie claps. "Ronan was so

concerned about that ankle of yours yesterday. He asked me to check on you. Sometimes Rocky can be a bit of a handful, but he's a mighty good dog and so lucky that Ronan rescued him."

My heart squeezes a bit at this. "Oh. It's nothing, really."

It seems, however, like a lot more than nothing. I hadn't expected Ronan to care. And he rescued Rocky. The speaks volumes of his kindness. My words from yesterday come back to haunt me.

The conversation turns to the best kind of ointment to use on poison oak, which Ms. Maggie apparently got while chasing a raccoon away from her little dog, Fluffy, yesterday. Since Ms. Maggie and Mom are highly invested in the various creams and oils, I use this as my escape to the sanctuary.

I'm fifteen minutes early, so I walk around to the side of the building and into the fenced-off preserve area. Outside the fence I see freshly cleaned buckets stacked along the edge from what I assume was the morning feeding. The scent of oats and grain is still heavy in the air. Dr. Allen told us that Ranger Anderson oversees the sanctuary, but he didn't mention who the tech manager is.

A horse's neigh echoes in the stillness. We couldn't visit the stable grounds yesterday, so I follow the fence around to get my first look. The stable stands out in bold red with white edging. A white wooden cross hangs just above the sliding doors. The smell of hay provides a comfort that sends me back to the stables at Great Bear. I've been riding horses since I was five, and it's second nature to me at this point. I would often go on trail rides through the rainforest with my parents and our community.

There's no one in sight, so I walk into the stable. It looks like all the horses have been turned out into the field. The stalls have fresh bedding, hay, and full water buckets. This lightens my heart and assures me that the sanctuary is well-run. There are bridles, harnesses, and lead ropes hanging on hooks by each stall. I count eight in all, with four on each side. All the doors are open except the last one on the right.

I walk to the back stall. A black-and-white Paint horse with bright blue eyes paws at the ground. He's about fifteen hands high (about five-feet at the shoulder) with a sturdy, compact build. The breed has long been a favorite of mine. We had Paint horses in Great Bear over the years, and I love their unique coloring. I would watch as the research team rode them into the forest for their field work. The horses often carried large amounts of scientific equipment on their strong backs. I've never seen one with two blue eyes though. One blue eye was common among our herd but never two. It really is a remarkable sight. The blue is so crystal clear, reminding me of one of the deep pools at the bottom of the many tiny waterfalls scattered throughout the rainforest.

His eyes assess me. What does he see in me?

Dad's words come back to me. "Horses can read people. They have the ability to reflect our emotions back to us."

The horse bobs his head twice and then continues chewing his hay, comfortable with my presence. The name Cosmo stands out in bright-white print above his bridle hook. Whoever picked it made a good choice for this guy. His eyes seem to reflect a million stars. I click my tongue, and his ears perk up, twitching in my direction.

"Hey Cosmo," I murmur to him. "It's okay. Just saying hi."

He takes a few steps closer, stopping just out of reach. I stretch out my hand, and he gently nuzzles it. His whiskers tickle my palm. I've missed this so much. I lean closer to him and inhale the earthy horse scent.

"I see you've already met Cosmo."

I jump back, causing Cosmo to retreat to the rear of the stall. Ronan stands there watching us.

"I was just leaving," I murmur, walking as quickly as I can out of the stable.

"Where are you going?" Ronan calls after me.

"I'm meeting the tech manager, so you can get back to whatever you were doing," I call back as more of a plea than anything else.

I don't give him a chance to answer, and I hurry back to the entrance of the sanctuary.

What's wrong with me? Why do I get so defensive around Ronan?

Papa Jay's words come to mind. "Hurt people, hurt others." His words never seemed truer than now.

The sanctuary door is still closed, and my watch reads 9:15. I'm beginning to wonder if the tech manager is ever going to show up. Then I see Ronan walking toward me again. I groan. He continues up on the porch, ducking slightly under the curved rooftop, and that's when I notice his T-shirt reads "Redwood Hills Animal Sanctuary."

It can't be.

"Sadie Foster? Welcome to the Redwood Hills Animal Sanctuary. I'm Ronan O'Connor, the tech manager," he says with a lopsided smile.

I don't know whether to laugh or cry.

I FOLLOW Ronan inside the lodge, and I'm immediately hit with the scent of lemon cleaner. Wildlife photos hang in black frames on the walls, and I'm immediately drawn to one. It's a close-up of a grey wolf standing on a large rock, staring up into the twinkling night sky. From his slightly-turned head, golden eyes reflect the moonlight, creating a harmony between him and the forest. There's a docile beauty to his features, all while maintaining a certain edge of alertness and pride. It's the perfect blend of incredible strength and undeniable vulnerability.

I feel Ronan watching me. "It's a beautiful photo."

He shrugs. "It's easy to take a beautiful photo when the subject is beautiful."

"You took this photo?"

"Yeah," he replies rather sheepishly. "Kind of a hobby of mine."

I look around the walls again with a new perspective. The photos stare back at me, each capturing the beauty of the creature. The photos reflect the photographer as much as they capture the animal.

"They're all your photos?" I ask.

Ronan shrugs again as he puts his hands in his jean pockets. I stroll around the room to get a better look at the other photos. Studying the images is like seeing Ronan for the first time.

After a few minutes, Ronan walks to the front desk. "I'm going to get the computer up and running to show you the employee technician program."

I pull myself away from the photos and join him. A brand-new Mac desktop sits on the large pine desk. How often did we request funds for new computers at Great Bear? We had wanted Macs for their research and database capability, but without the proper funding, we had to stay with a more outdated program and computer package. Dr. Allen seems to have the newest and best of everything.

Ronan shows me "Animal Care," the program that keeps track of the technician's hours and daily assignments. I admit that it is a technical advancement compared to ours at Great Bear. Now I understand why Mom was gushing over the veterinary center.

"Tablets are assigned to the techs to log all animal feedings, medications, and observations." He hands me a shiny tablet enclosed in a heavy-duty black case. "There's an Animal Care app too. I've already downloaded it for you."

I log into the app with my new credentials and follow along as Ronan shows me how to set up my account. My name already appears as a technician. The photo beside it is blank, but I can see the other technician's photos. Ronan's profile is at the top with "manager" in red underneath. His photo is a close-up of him with a grey wolf pup. The pup looks so tiny curled up next to his broad chest. His muscled arms hold it in a tender hug. He's wearing a faded red sanctuary hoodie, and his Giants hat is turned backward, covering most of his hair so that just a few dark strands stick out around his ears. The cub looks up at him with admiration in its eyes, as Ronan gives an easy smile at the camera. His affection for the pup does things to my heart that I've never felt before.

"And here is your bag," Ronan says, interrupting my thoughts. He hands me a thick, tan canvas belt bag with the green Redwood Hills Animal Sanctuary logo embroidered on the center. I unzip the main compartment and slide the tablet inside.

"The bags are new," Ronan explains, as if reading my mind. "They are waterproof and keep us hands-free in the habitats. It was Gia's idea. Since she's Dr. Allen's niece, she helped to get him to pay for them all."

I smile remembering Gia's undeniable energy and warmth. "I met Gia last night at the diner. She's nice."

"Yeah, she is."

A twinge of jealousy hits. Where did that come from?

He hands me a key on a leather fob stitched with the logo. "Key to the lodge, which will give you access to all the other keys for the habitats, supplies, and stuff." I put the key in the small, zippered pocket of the bag.

There are two offices on each side of the lobby area. The larger one is Ranger Anderson's office, and the smaller one is Ronan's office. Walking into Ranger Anderson's office is like walking into a mess, really. The room is spacious, with walls painted in steel blue, offsetting the wooden log furniture. A large pine desk, covered with papers, sits on a worn, golden area rug. A faded, navy work jacket hangs on the back of the distressed brown chair while a pair of thick, well-worn work gloves sit on a stack of manila envelopes. A large double window on the side of the room provides natural light, highlighting the plaid sofa of green, red, and gold against the wall. A large cream-colored wool blanket is spread out on the couch. A portion is balled up like it was recently slept on.

On the wall behind the desk is a large, exquisite photo of a mountain lion lying on a rock formation with its front paws crossed. There's a calm peace in its posture, but the eyes are sharp and focused. It's the look of an animal comfortable in its own skin but always alert. This mountain lion is a protector. Beneath the calm is a spirit of steel. This is one of Ronan's photos. I can feel it. Without even knowing Ranger Anderson, it's like I understand him. It's clear that Ronan has a special gift for seeing people and animals for who they are.

He walks over to the desk and pushes a wildlife guide off the edge. "Colin runs the sanctuary but spends most of his time out in the field. And don't worry, it looks like a mess in here, but he has a 'system.' Believe me, he's said it a million times. He has a reason for doing everything that he does. We help him with maintaining the habitats and occasionally with rescues, but he has always worked closely with the wildlife vet."

Ronan's office is smaller but much more organized than Ranger Anderson's. His ceiling curves more on the side, creating a hideaway for a large built-in window and bookcase on each side. The shelves hold field guides, animal behavior and anatomy books, wildlife encyclopedias, and various parks resources. A battered, leather-bound edition of Jack London's *The Call of the Wild* sits on the edge of a shelf. I run my finger over the worn cover and resist the urge to open it and begin reading. It was one of the first books Dad and I read together.

Ronan's log desk is similar to Ranger Anderson's but built into the wall. The curve of the desk gives a spectacular view of the woods through the open window. There isn't much wall space. There are no photos hanging in his office, which seems odd since this is the only place in the building where his work is absent. I envision a woven tapestry that would be perfect for his wall.

His desk is neat and organized. A few folders are stacked to one side. A black printer sits to the other side with paper full in the tray. On top of a large planner is the rolled-up *National Geographic* from yesterday. I resist the urge to take it, and instead I pick up a silver photo frame. It's a photo of Ronan, three children, and Rocky sitting around a bonfire.

"Are these your brothers and sister?"

"Yeah." Ronan looks over my shoulder. He smells of light pine and roast coffee. "That's Declan. He's ten. Liam's eight, and Maeve is six."

As he points to each of them, I hear a tenderness in his voice. The photo of Ronan and the wolf pup flashes in my mind. It's obvious he loves them very much.

"And, well, you already met Rocky," he says quietly.

"I'm sorry." The words come out before I know what I'm saying. "It wasn't him. He just caught me at a bad moment. You both did."

Ronan looks at me with the same concern he had yesterday, and nods slightly. "I'm sorry too. It was a long day, and I wasn't in the best mood."

I put the photo back on his desk. "I get it."

He opens the planner and schedules me to tour the sanctuary and habitats on Friday. "After the tour, you can begin shadowing me and the other techs."

"I wish I could start now."

"I know the feeling. Being at the sanctuary is always the best part of my day. I'll update the Animal Care system later on, and you'll be able to see the schedule on the app."

"Thanks. I'll check it out."

He closes the planner with a nod, and a new energy fills the space between us.

"Gia told me about the movie night at school tomorrow," I mention casually, as we walk to the front door. "She wants me to meet up with her. I was thinking about it, but I'm not sure."

His silence lasts a moment too long. I reach for the door handle, but Ronan opens it for me instead.

"You should go."

I freeze at his abruptness.

"To the movie, I mean," he quickly clarifies. "It'll be fun, and I'll see you there."

My face warms as I smile at him for the first time. Walking back to the research center, thoughts of Ronan and tomorrow night fill my thoughts. I pull out my phone and finally call Anna.

She answers on the first ring. "Hey, Sadie!"

"Anna, there's a boy, and I think I might be falling for him."

CHAPTER FOUR

It's Friday evening, and my body is full of nerves as I consider what the night may bring. I run my fingers through my hair to loosen the curls that fall about midway down my back. I slip on my yellow cotton sundress and add long, golden leaf earrings. Carefully I clip my gold bear-paw necklace around my neck, feeling the weight of the metal on my chest. It's the first time I've worn the necklace since my dad's death.

I pull on my hiking boots and grab my brown leather bag, sliding the strap across my shoulder. After a brief search of the hall closet, I find our red-and-white plaid picnic blanket. Tossing the blanket and my bag into the Jeep, I wait for Mom.

The ride to the school is quiet. Mom keeps shooting worried glances my way, and I look out the window to avoid her eyes, opting to put on my much-practiced strong face. I pretend that I couldn't care less about this movie night, when of course, that couldn't be further from the truth.

As we pull into the parking lot, the field is already packed with people. Blankets line the field, and groups of teenagers toss beach balls through the air. There's a concession stand selling popcorn and candy with a long line already forming along the side.

"Well, this looks fun." Mom leans out of the window to get a better look. When I don't reply, she gives my arm a little rub and eyes my necklace. She blinks back tears. "Try to enjoy yourself, Sadie."

"Sure." I climb out of the Jeep, shutting the door with more force than I intend.

"Have fun!" It's that forced cheerful voice again, but I see her worried expression in the rearview mirror.

"Sadie!" Gia runs up the hill to me. "Come on! We're all set up."

Gia looks adorable in her short, blue-and-white Hawaiian sundress and white sandals. Her long, straight black hair is pulled back into a ponytail and tied with a bright blue ribbon. A yellow-flowered lei hangs around her neck. With her dark sunglasses and bright pink lipstick, she looks more like a model for some Caribbean resort than a high school junior.

I follow Gia to the field and lay my blanket next to hers. She talks to everyone walking by, and I wonder if there's anyone who she doesn't know. She's clearly well-liked, and I can see why.

"Hua!" Gia calls, and a tall girl with long, shiny black hair and beautiful almond-shaped eyes runs over to us. She wraps Gia in a hug, and they laugh.

Gia points to me. "This is Sadie. She's new this year. Her mom works with Uncle Eric."

Hua's eyes light up. "So nice to meet you, Sadie!" She wraps me in a hug, like I'm an old friend.

"You, too. I'm excited for this year."

Hua smiles. "It's going to be the best year yet!"

"No doubt," Gia agrees.

"Oh, it's Conrad. I'll catch up with you guys later!" Hua runs off into the crowd.

"Hua and Conrad have been dating for two years. Cutest couple in the school."

Gia introduces me to what feels like the entire school by the time the movie begins. I have forgotten just about everybody's name, and I'm staying close to Gia because the place is getting packed. Apparently, this is the last big blowout before school starts on Monday. I never imagined that there would be this many people, and the one person who I haven't seen is unfortunately the one I was most hoping to see. An image of Ronan's caramel eyes flashes through my mind.

The Marvel theme song blares from the speakers, and everyone begins cheering. The movie begins as Thor hangs by ropes and banters with the dragon.

"Hey."

I jump at his voice. "Oh, hey."

I move over, and he takes a seat beside me. "I didn't think you were coming."

"You were looking for me, huh?" A teasing smile plays on his lips.

"No." My denial is weak, and it's obvious.

"I had to stay late to help Colin close the racoon enclosure." Concern is evident in his eyes.

"Are the racoons okay?" I ask.

"Yeah, they're fine. It was more that Colin and Dr. Allen got into it about something, and I've never seen Colin so angry. He grabbed a flashlight and went into the woods, leaving me to finish the racoon's meds."

"The woods?"

"Anytime Colin needs to think he heads for the woods."

Ranger Anderson and I have at least one thing in common. The woods are where I've always gone too.

"What were they fighting about?"

Ronan shrugs. "No idea."

Before he can say more, a girl slides in next to Ronan, pushing the two of us so close our arms are now touching. Ronan smiles down at me, eyebrows raised. My nerves get the better of me, and I move over to put some space between us. Now I'm sitting half on the blanket and half in the grass.

The girl next to Ronan turns my way, and I immediately recognize her as the hostess from the diner. Her dark hair hangs straight above her shoulders, showing off the white of her tank top and tanned skin. She's one person that Gia hasn't introduced me to tonight.

"Hey," Gia says, leaning over to me. "Wanna get some popcorn?"

"Yes!" I would grab any opportunity to talk to Gia right now.

As we walk away, I turn to Gia. "I think I saw that girl the other day at the diner." I try to sound as nonchalant as I can, but I'm failing terribly.

"Who? Callie?"

"Is she the one sitting by Ronan?" I ask.

"Yup. She's a hostess at the diner."

"Yeah, that's right." I pause to think of what to say next. "This probably sounds weird, but I feel like she was staring at me when we were there. But I'm sure it was just my imagination."

"Probably not." Gia laughs. "She can be a little standoffish at first, but she's a lot of fun once you get to know her—that is, if you can get her away from Ronan. She has it bad for him."

My stomach sinks. Of course he has a girlfriend. "So they are together?"

"Nah. They went out a few times last year, but it didn't last. She's been trying to get together with him ever since though. I feel bad for her. She really needs to move on. There are plenty of guys who are into her, but she's only interested in Ronan." Gia shrugs and grabs a bag of popcorn and a soda.

As I reach for my popcorn and soda, I notice an intense sense of relief come over me, which is odd considering I've only talked to Ronan a few times, half of which was me yelling at him. But I can't deny my relief. We head back to the blankets with our popcorn, stopping every few feet to talk to another friend of Gia.

When we reach the blankets, I notice that Callie has moved closer to Hua, and Ronan has moved over a little, giving me more room to sit. I gladly take my seat back and offer him some popcorn. The butter is still warm.

We're about halfway through the movie when Gia stands and stretches her arms above her head. "Alright, who's ready for some volleyball?" She nods to the back of the field.

There's a large group of students playing what looks more like a fierce game of dodgeball with beach balls than any volleyball game I've ever seen.

"I'm going to pass this time," I tell her, not sure that I'm up for anymore socializing.

Callie grabs Ronan's arm and attempts to pull him up with her, but he doesn't budge. I try my best to avert my eyes but fail miserably. Callie leans in close and whispers something in Ronan's ear. He shakes his head and says something back, but it's too quiet to hear.

I lean closer to catch a bit of their conversation but stop when I catch Gia giving me a funny look. Straightening back up, I pretend to be engrossed in the movie instead of eavesdropping. Callie runs her hand over Ronan's back one last time before getting up. Ronan doesn't show any response, and she shoots me a heated look as she walks away.

"You have any popcorn left?" Ronan asks with that side smile I remember from the first day we met.

I put the bucket between us, and his hand brushes mine as we both reach at the same time. Our hands stay a moment longer than necessary, and I imagine what it would be like to hold his hand. My thoughts wander that path until I notice he's staring at me with a raised eyebrow.

"What?"

"I was just asking if you like Thor?" An amused expression plays on his face.

"Who?"

"Thor, you know, the superhero in the movie we're watching."

"Oh." I pause. "Yeah, sure. Of course. You?" I ask, sounding just as awkward as I feel.

"Ragnarök is the best in the series. But I've always been more of a Captain America guy."

I'm not sure what to say since I haven't watched any of these movies before. I'm feeling the distance between our two worlds. Things were so different in Great Bear, and this is all so new. Not good or bad—just different. A sudden gust of wind comes out of nowhere, and the popcorn begins flying from the bucket. Ronan attempts to stop the bucket from blowing away, but he accidentally knocks it over instead. Pieces of popcorn blow around us as we try to catch them, like children trying to catch bubbles in the air.

I hear the voices and laughter of people around us, but their words are just a muffled soundtrack. It feels so good to laugh. A real laugh. Ronan leans toward me. His fingers graze my cheek, leaving a warm trail behind. When I look up, I see confusion in his eyes.

"Got one," he says. His voice is deeper than normal. He shows me the piece of popcorn that he retrieved from my hair.

As much as I want to laugh again and keep the friendly conversation going, I can't. I know how much I wanted him to kiss me, which terrifies me. Ronan drops the popcorn on the ground and looks back to the screen.

As the closing credits begin, Gia and Callie come back talking about a bonfire at Evan's house. I kind of remember meeting Evan, but everyone has blended at this point. The last thing I want to do is be around more people tonight though. I'm so drained from the day. I just want to get into my pajamas for some much-needed sleep.

"I think I'm just going to go back," I tell Gia. "Don't worry about taking me home. I'll call my mom. She'll come and get me."

I catch the crooked smile on Callie's face.

"No worries, Sadie. I'll take you home before Evan's. But are you sure you don't want to come?"

"I can take her home." Ronan's voice stops us both. "I'm heading home myself, and my house is right next door."

Next door?

An image of the cabin I saw through the trees that first night comes to mind. The two-story dark wood cabin with a green metal roof. That must be his.

"Oh yeah, that makes sense. Is it okay with you, Sadie?" They all look at me.

"Sure." I twist the hem of my dress. "As long as you don't mind."

"Not at all." His eyes are smiling now.

"Okay, I'll give you a call tomorrow," Gia says in that carefree way of hers. She pulls Callie along with her to join the group heading to the bonfire.

Ronan rolls up my blanket and carries it for me. I have never been in a boy's car before. Well, I rode with Jason, Anna's brother, but that hardly counts. Ronan leads me to a faded black Dodge Ram. It's older and more beat-up than the new white one I saw him and Ranger Anderson using at the research center.

He opens the door for me, and I hop up onto the seat. His truck is as neat and clean as his office. It has the same light pine scent I now associate with Ronan. Hiking boots sit on the floor, and the sanctuary's tech bag is on the backseat.

He turns on the headlights, and I think back to my drive here. Could Ronan have been in the truck behind us that first night in the storm? I try to visualize the pickup truck that honked at us.

"Thanks for the ride." I click my seatbelt on.

"Anytime."

He slowly makes his way out of the parking lot, following the traffic guides and avoiding the crowd of people, which appears to be an Olympic feat. A few guys bang on the hood of the truck and call to Ronan. When we finally make it out of the parking lot, the back road brings back the memory of the drive to Redwood.

"I remember a dark truck behind us the night we moved here. It was during a bad storm."

A look flashes across Ronan's face. Recognition? Embarrassment?

"Was that you?" I ask him. "I mean, I heard you say you live close, and I was just wondering."

"Yeah, I realized the next day when I saw your Jeep parked outside the research center," he says sheepishly. Silence hangs for a moment before Ronan looks over at me. "Why were you stopped in the middle of the road? I thought maybe you were stuck or something."

The panic comes without warning, tightening its fingers around my throat. We were stopped in the middle of the road because I was lost in a memory that never seems to leave. I don't want him or anyone else to know the truth about what happened.

"Do you live in the cabin next to ours? The one on the other side of the trees?

He raises an eyebrow at my change of subject, but doesn't mention it. "Yeah. My dad and Colin built the cabin right before I was born. We've been there ever since."

I remember Mom saying that people take a lot of pride in building their cabins here. It's a legacy for many families. I can imagine it builds strong bonds among families. "Are Ranger Anderson and your dad good friends?"

Ronan's jaw clenches. "They used to be. But my dad isn't the same person he was then. He left us about 3 years ago. It's just me, my mom, and my siblings."

The hurt is raw in his voice, and I can't imagine how awful this must have been for Ronan. How does a father just leave his family? It gives new meaning to his relationship with Ranger Anderson though. It must be why they are so close now.

"I'm sorry. That must have been hard."

"We're better off without him."

I sense Ronan doesn't want to say anymore, and I don't push him. The truck bumps along the lane, and he slows down when we approach his cabin on the right. Rocky is standing on the front porch. His tail swings wildly at the sound of the truck.

"I've gotta pick Rocky up. If he hears the truck, and I don't stop, he'll just chase after it." He pulls to a stop. "I guess you weren't completely wrong about the training," he says with a chastened smile, and I can't help but laugh.

As soon as Rocky sees Ronan open the door, he begins to whine. It takes all of his effort to stay on the porch.

"Come on, boy!"

Ronan's large chocolate lab comes bounding toward the truck. He jumps up into the tailgate in one fluid motion. His joyful whimpering echoes in the night. Ronan climbs back into the truck, shaking his head. He looks just as happy as Rocky sounds. We drive the short distance to my house, and Ronan puts the truck in park. It's 10:30, but Mom isn't home yet. I check my phone, and there are no messages from her either—just one from Anna asking how the night went.

I drop my phone back into my bag and search for the cabin key.

"You, okay?"

"Yeah, I just realized I left my key in my room. It's okay though, my mom will be home soon. I'll just wait on the porch."

"I'll wait with you."

"You don't need to."

"I want to."

My heart flutters as Rocky prances beside me up to the porch. Ronan and I each take a rocking chair, and Rocky lies by my feet. The crickets chirp in the long grass, and there's a gentle, cool breeze now—not the wind gusts we had earlier at school.

"Did you have a chance to meet people tonight?" Ronan asks. "I'm sure Gia introduced you to some of her friends, right?"

"I think she introduced me to everyone in the school. I barely remember three names. Yours is one of them."

He laughs. "That sounds about right."

"It's just so much," I explain. "All the people and everything. I'm not sure what I expected, but somehow this wasn't it."

"Is it really that different from your old school?"

"I don't have an old school. Well, not like yours I mean. I was homeschooled on the research base in Great Bear. This is my first time going to a school."

He doesn't say anything at first. I don't know if he somehow knows that I'm uncomfortable talking about it or if he just doesn't know what to say.

"What do you think so far?" he finally asks, breaking the silence. "I mean, I know it was just a movie night, but are you happy you're here?"

I sigh and think for a moment. That's a loaded question—one that I'm not sure how to answer.

"I don't know. It's exciting but scary at the same time, you know? Like the movie tonight—it was exciting to see Gia and meet her friends and everything, and it was nice watching the movie," I say, shooting him a quick glance, "but I was also thinking about how I just wanted to be home."

An image of Great Bear comes to mind—the deep greens of the forest and cool breezes off of the sea. There's a cool breeze tonight as well, but it feels different. It smells different. The scent of fish and moss is replaced with pine and the mild spice of the redwoods. I'm not sure where my home is anymore.

"Home here or in Great Bear?" Ronan asks, as if reading my mind.

He gets it. "Honestly, I'm not sure."

His eyes are soft and intent on me. "Well, Rocky's glad you're here."

My laugh causes Rocky's head to shoot up. His amber eyes fill with undeniable love. I rub behind his ears, and he lays his head on my lap, with his tongue hanging out the side of his mouth.

"You're one of a kind," I tell Rocky, kissing his big head.

"Funny, I was thinking the same about you."

There's a teasing smile on his lips, but his eyes are serious. Heat prickles my cheeks, and I tuck a strand of hair behind my ear.

Just then headlights shine down the lane. Mom pulls into our driveway, stopping next to Ronan's truck.

And just like that the night is over. But somehow I know that something else is just beginning.

THREE DAYS LATER, Mom and I drive in silence to Redwood Academy. It's the first day of school, and the gravity of the situation is weighing heavily on both of us. I look down at my light blue cotton sundress with navy blue birds. I embroidered the wings to look like they are at different stages of flight. I pull my white jean jacket close. The cool wind blows through my long curls as we round the bend to school.

"Good luck today." Mom leans over and kisses my cheek.

"Thanks. You, too. First day of regular office appointments is a big deal."

"I know. I like the idea of have regular clients in addition to the research center." She pulls on a stray curl by her temple—a clue to her excitement.

"I'll see you after school."

I watch the Jeep drive away before walking across the parking lot. Keeping my eyes forward, I walk toward the entrance. A few people give a "hello," but most just stare at me.

"Hey, Sadie!" Gia pops up next to me. I'm so grateful for her presence that I almost hug her right in the parking lot.

"Relax." She wraps her arm in mine. "Listen, by this point they've all either met you at the movie night or heard about you. They just want to see you now. Not everyone was at the movie night, and this school doesn't get new students very often. Believe me, I've been through it. I was that new girl last year. After a few days, your newness will wear off, and no one will notice. Although with the way you look, I'm thinking the guys will still notice."

I fidget with the button on the cuff of my jean jacket.

Gia waves to a group of people, and we begin walking their way. Luckily, I recognize them from the movie night. While the group is talking about teachers and new classes, I wonder where Ronan could be.

And then, as if on cue, I see him. Ronan is leaning against his truck with his hands in his jean pockets. He isn't wearing his hat, and his messy hair looks damp, like he just got out of the shower. I can almost smell his pine scent. I'm taking in his worn Redwood Hills Baseball T-shirt when our eyes lock.

I jump as a hand touches my shoulder.

"Hey, Sadie! What's your schedule look like?"

One of the boys in the group looks expectantly at me. He's familiar from the movie night, and I place him as Evan, the guy who had the bonfire party. I show him the schedule I'm holding in my sweaty hand.

"Awesome. We have American Lit and PE together. PE with Coach Griffen will be awesome, but we'll be trying to stay awake in Mrs. Gentry's Lit class. Hua had her for Lit. She said it's where she perfected the open-eyed nap." He does a funny imitation of Hua.

"Oh wow, that sounds interesting, or maybe not."

Evan laughs. Out of the corner of my eye, I notice Ronan watching us.

"Coach Griffen is the baseball coach, right?" How I remembered that from all the conversations during the movie night I don't know. Actually I do know. Ronan is on the baseball team.

"Yeah, he's the best. This is his tenth-year coaching, and he has had winning seasons the past nine years. We've got a good chance for another championship this year too. You'll have to come out and watch our games."

"That sounds fun." It surprises me that I really mean it. Evan's so easy to talk to. Cute too. He's tall with sandy blond hair and blue eyes.

Evan's face lights up. "Actually, we're having a Fall Festival in a couple weeks. You can't miss it. The team does it every year as a fundraiser. Anyone can play in the pick-up game, and Ms. Maggie makes her famous apple pie. But I'd wait to go on the rides afterward if I were you."

I imagine that Ms. Maggie's pie is as interesting as every other part of her. "I'll remember that."

"It's always a great day." Evan grins, and I feel myself grinning back. "I'm sure you'd have a blast. If you want, you could come with me, and we could—"

"Hey."

The air between us immediately thickens.

"Ronan! What's up, man? I was just telling Sadie about the Fall Festival."

Evan gives him a good-natured high five while Ronan looks at me.

"Sadie, you planning on going?" Ronan asks. His eyes have an intensity that I haven't seen in them before.

"I don't know," I reply.

"Come on," Evan says playfully. "It's the best way to start the year."

"Sure, that sounds fun." I force a smile.

Thunder rumbles in Ronan's eyes as I give Evan my phone number. Then, I walk with Gia into the school for the very first time.

MY FIRST CLASS of the day is biology. I choose a seat near the front and against the side window where there aren't many people. My thoughts keep wandering back to Ronan. Was he jealous that I gave Evan my number?

Things are changing so quickly. This move is completely changing my life, and I'm not sure how to handle everything.

Ronan appears at the classroom door. He chooses the empty seat diagonally behind me.

"Hey, Sadie."

I turn around just as another guy comes over to Ronan's desk talking about baseball. Ronan unenthusiastically answers his questions, glancing at me every few seconds. The annoyance on his face is obvious, but this guy is oblivious.

When he finally leaves, I feel Ronan lean toward me.

"Hey." His smile doesn't quite reach his eyes. "You and Evan are going to the festival together?"

I shrug. "Yeah, I guess. Are you going to be there?"

"Yeah. The team plays in the game. The whole school will be there."

"Do you think I shouldn't go with Evan?" My heart pounds in my throat.

I catch a hopeful look in his eyes before his face hardens. "Ah, no, Evan's a good guy. We've been friends for a long time."

My stomach drops. He had his chance, and he didn't take it. We look at each other for another moment before a young woman in her early thirties walks into the classroom carrying a canvas tote bag in hand and a Redwood Academy coffee mug in the other. Her ginger hair flows in loose waves just past her shoulders. Her dark green glasses illuminate her blue eyes. She's dressed in a white cotton dress with a long, green cardigan and brown sandals.

"Good morning!" She places her tote on the large, empty desk and pulls a hardcover book from the tote. "Please raise your hand when you hear your name."

After a long attendance check, consisting of three mispronunciations and two students in the wrong classroom, class finally begins.

"Well now that half of the class is over, let's get started," Ms. Hannon quips, and there's a rumble of laughter in the room.

"Junior year biology. Who's excited?" She winks at the class. "Our curriculum requires students to study physics before biology to gain some fundamental knowledge about life science. The physics and chemistry you took part in the past two years has prepared you for this. I guarantee that by the end of the year you will find an area of life science that speaks to you as we see some of the most incredible organisms come to life before us."

Her gaze then settles on me. My neck tingles as I feel her eyes assessing me. I sit up straighter in my chair and look out the window. Her lecture continues, and I glance at the schedule on my desk. Textiles, my art elective, is my last period of the day. I am looking forward to this class the most. I love making clothing and feel best in my handmade dresses—with hiking boots of course.

"We will even touch on the topic of the infamous Kermode bear, otherwise known as the spirit bear."

My body freezes at Ms. Hannon's words, and all thoughts of art scatter from my mind.

"They are an interesting species—one that is often misunderstood. If you've ever felt misunderstood, you might find a friend in them." There is no mistaking the look she sends me.

My ears start to ring and block out Ms. Hannon's words as she continues. It's like she's talking right to me. The images of that day in the woods flash through my mind—Dad's body lying motionless in the mud and the poacher's footsteps fading into the trees. I slide down in my seat. My hands tighten into fists, and my body goes into survival mode.

My eyes dart around the room expecting to see everyone staring at me, but to my amazement, no one is looking at me. I slowly flex my fingers, trying to loosen them. The guy to my right scribbles in his notebook. The girl across from him looks forward but nods off every few seconds before her head snaps up. Others seem to be intent on Ms. Hannon and take notes. Trying to regain my balance, I force my breathing to slow, and my fists relax. I slowly close my eyes and start counting down. Ten, nine, eight, seven, six, five, four, three, two...

I jump at the ring of the bell and quickly gather my books, dropping a couple pencils in the process. Rushing toward the door, I hit my knee on a desk leg. I bite down from the pain and force myself to keep moving, pushing past Ronan on the way. Out of the corner of my eye, Ronan is watching me, questions burning in his eyes.

CHAPTER FIVE

The school week flies, and by last period on Friday, I can honestly say that while it has been a hard adjustment, textiles makes it all worth it.

Ms. Auclair shakes a little bell to signal the beginning of class. The Art Wing is a new addition to the school that was finished just a few weeks ago, and the school bell cannot be heard yet. There's something nice about being separated from the rest of the school this way.

"Today we are going to choose a project for the semester. It is up to you to decide what your project will be. Then, if I approve your project, it will serve as your independent work this semester. I encourage you to find something you love and make it your own! Go on now and start creating!"

Ms. Auclair does a little twirl, and her red-and-purple whimsical dress spins. With her petite stature, dark pixie cut, and eccentric earrings, she gives off a fun vibe. She recently graduated from an art college in New York City and has an energy that makes me want to absorb every word she says about fibers and permeability.

I pull out my sketchbook and open to a blank page. I tap my pencil, hoping for an idea to come.

"Sadie, what ideas have you come up with?" Ms. Auclair leans over my sketchbook.

I try to cover the blankness with my hand. "I'm still thinking."

She pulls up a stool beside me, and the scent of oil paint and honeysuckle fills the space. "Maybe begin with your intention for the project. Is there a need you wish to fill?"

My expression is as blank as the page.

"When I was first given an assignment like this, I was a bit lost too. It was my junior year in high school, just like you. My older brother was recently accepted into the college of his choice, and I was upset because Colorado was a long way from our home in upstate New York. He was my best friend after our parents' divorce, and I couldn't bear the thought of him not being around. So I decided to make him a wall quilt to take with him to college. He always loved baseball, so I made each square to represent a different team." Her eyes take on a far-away look before she continues. "Anyway, I made the quilt for him because I knew it would be meaningful to him, and in the process, it healed a part of my heart as well."

"I bet he loves it."

"He did. Sadly, he passed away two years ago. A car accident."

"I'm so sorry."

She runs a hand through her hair. "It's okay. We don't know why things happen the way they do, but there's meaning to be found in any situation. Today, the quilt hangs on the wall of his son's bedroom. My little nephew treasures that quilt more than I could've ever imagined."

"I'm sure he does."

"Sometimes when we create something, we not only show someone how much we care but also how they have changed our life—how they bring love into our hearts."

She walks over to check another student's book. The story of her brother is still in my mind as I begin sketching on the white paper.

AFTER SCHOOL, I go to the animal sanctuary to tour the animal habitats with Ronan and Ranger Anderson.

"You ready?" Ronan asks when I finish signing in.

"So ready. I can't believe how many different species are being cared for at the sanctuary."

"We've really built something here. The current animals are all listed in the Animal Care app with photos and care plans." There's pride in Ronan's voice.

I open the Animal Care app and scroll down to the list of animals.

ACTIVE ANIMALS WITH CARE PLANS
Bobcat (2 females)
River otter (2 males, 1 female)
Porcupine (1 male)
Pacific shrew (2 males, 2 females)
Mountain beaver (1 male, 1 female)
Californian vole (3 males)
Roosevelt elk (1 male)
Mink (1 female)
Weasel (1 male)
Raccoon (4 females)
Chipmunk (2 females)
Northern spotted owl (1 male, 1 female)
California condor (1 male)
Black bear (1 female, recently released, currently tracking)

I stop scrolling and click on the link for the black bear's statistics. *Injured female (gunshot wound), rehabilitated and released. Tracking: consistent movement. No reports of new injuries or events.*

I exit out of the animal care list and click on the stable icon. There's a separate area on the app to record the care of the horses, and I've spent a lot of time reading the notes recently. The horses are all rescues who have been rehabilitated and are used for fieldwork with the research team, just like at Great Bear. Ranger Anderson said that some go up for adoption when the time is right or when they receive another rescue. They keep eight horses at a time on the base.

Cosmo's photo stares back at me. Cosmo was an abuse case, like most of the others. He was severely neglected and worked to the bone before Ranger Anderson and the team rescued him. There's a pending court case coming up in a few weeks, and it will determine legal rights of ownership. Just the thought of someone harming an animal infuriates me. Cosmo is recovering from a mild strained tendon in his front right leg, by the cannon bone. He was just recently released back into the field. His medical exam was what kept Mom out so late the during the movie night.

I love being around the animals but also love being a part of something that is bigger than any one animal—something improving the lives of so many.

Ranger Anderson joins us. He's holding a tablet and a medical bag. "I thought we could start with the California condor. He's one of our newer rescues but should be cleared for release soon. You wouldn't want to miss seeing him."

"Sounds good to me."

We walk around the corner of the lodge to the Avian enclosure. A variety of penned cages cover a two-acre space. Ranger Anderson and Ronan move through the maintenance and operating procedures flawlessly, as if they work better as a unit than separate. It's interesting to watch them together. In one way they are like a father and son team, but there's such a strong friendship there too. There's a deep respect in their interactions.

When we arrive at the enclosure, I hadn't expected the immense size of the bird. "Is it safe?"

"It's one of the largest flying birds in the world," Ranger Anderson says. "Their wings can span nine feet, and they usually weigh around twenty pounds. All animals have the potential to inflict harm if they feel threatened, but this guy is very cooperative. We will keep the beak tie on though, just to be safe."

Ronan pulls on his heavy canvas jacket and gloves. "Condors will often let other birds, like the Golden Eagle feed first, so they appear gentler. But a female protecting her nest is fierce."

I examine the huge bird from a few feet away. He's looking at me with round, black eyes and turning his head slightly, as if examining me as well. He is tied to the perch at the ankle, with about a foot of loose, coated chain dangling off the perch for movement.

"He reminds me of a vulture." His naked pink head with black feathers poking around the back like an ornamental headdress. Long smooth black feathers coat the rest of his body. He lifts one wing in a stretching movement, and I glimpse the white triangular-striped feathers underneath.

Ronan stands next to me while Ranger Anderson retrieves the feed bucket. "They are both scavenging birds. Condors can glide for hours looking for food, reaching up to fifty-five miles per hour. They look for large carcasses and recent kills while the meat is still fresh. Vultures aren't always so picky."

Ranger Anderson takes a slab of fresh meat from the bucket and coats it with a mineral supplement.

"Why was he rescued?" I ask.

Ranger Anderson shakes his head before answering. "Condors are critically endangered, mostly from habitat loss and lead poisoning. We found him very weak about three miles from here."

"How was he poisoned?" I wonder aloud.

"He was feeding on a deer carcass, and there was residual lead from a bullet. The exposure to lead shuts down organs and weakens muscles. He was on the brink of death when we found him, but he has a strong spirit."

"If a hunter shot the deer, why didn't he take it with him?" I ask.

Ranger Anderson and Ronan exchange disgusted looks.

"For sport. We see it all the time." Ronan clenches his jaw.

"So sad." I'm not new to hunting and have been on a few hunting trips with my parents, but we never killed for sport. We hunted for our food, and we were always particular about using the whole animal and not letting anything go to waste.

Ranger Anderson places the slab of meat on an adjacent platform, and the condor begins tearing it with his sharp, curved beak. It's both incredibly beautiful and disturbing to watch.

"Look who's here," a deep voice comes from behind us. The condor flaps its wings.

Ranger Anderson stiffens. "The feeding sign is on the door."

"Ah, yes. But Dr. Foster is here with me, and she's interested in watching our condor feed before clearing him for release."

Ranger Anderson glances at Mom. The iciness disappears, and a warmth comes into his eyes. "He's just finishing up."

"It never loses its beauty, does it?" She stands by Ranger Anderson.

"No, it doesn't."

Mom turns to me. "Sadie, this is something you may never see again. Take in these moments, and never let them go."

I nod unable to take my eyes off the bird.

After a few minutes, Ronan nudges me. "Can you hold these?"

He hands me his gloves and then pulls his camera out of a black bag. He begins snapping pictures from different angles until the condor finishes his meal.

I TAKE my break sitting by the flower garden next to the main lodge. My finger rolls over the wild lavender. The contrast of rough buds and soft petals is a favorite of mine. There is so much depth and delicacy. I envision a long-flowing muslin maxi dress, soft to the touch but with raised designs to bring out the natural dimensions.

I've always loved the art of design. I feel alive when I'm designing, much like Ronan when he's taking photos. He looked so alive in the condor enclosure today. One of those photos will end up on the wall of the sanctuary, and it will capture the essence of that moment and the spirit of the bird. It won't just hang on his office wall. Every time I think about Ronan's blank wall in his office, something doesn't seem right.

Just like that, I know what my textiles project should be. I pull out my sketchbook, relax in the chair, and draw until I drift off to sleep, allowing the dream to fill my mind.

Through the haze, salmonberry and foxglove fall to the ground. There's a fast movement through the trees. Branches crack on the ground. The sound of heavy breathing echoes in my ears. Angel comes through the opening in the trees. Her paws pound the hard ground. I run to catch up with her, with the sound of footsteps behind me. My lungs burn as I run side-by-side with her. Adrenaline pushes me forward. Sunlight streams through the spaces between the branches, creating a spotted aura around us. The footsteps are getting clos-

er. Behind us a large, dark shadow becomes visible around the bend. The shadow appears to run straight toward us. Its arms reach for a rifle that hangs across its body, and in doing so a bright glint reflects from the barrel. I urge Angel forward, running as quickly as we can over the logs and rocks. My foot catches on a rock, and I fall hard against the cold ground. "Keep running!" I yell to Angel. She stops and looks at me. Her deep brown eyes glisten with a mixture of compassion and primal fear. "Go," I beg her. "Run away." She gives me one last pained look before running away, as the dark shadow moves closer and closer.

I awake to the bright sunlight, with my heart pounding in my chest. My eyes dart around looking for any sign of the time or place. My mind is fuzzy, and I'm lightheaded as I try to stand.

What was that? The question screams in my mind. This dream was different than the first—more of a warning. The spirit bears are in danger, but it's more than that. We're all in danger. I can't shake this feeling that something bad is about to happen and I need to stop it.

But I've tried to help before, and I lost everything. I tried to help, and it led to Dad's death and our lives being completely changed forever.

I am not the one they need.

Mom and the research team could help. That's all I can do—warn them. I tell myself this would be enough, but a question lingers in my heart.

Why are you hiding?

I go into the side entrance of the veterinary clinic to talk to Mom. I stop just out the exam room door when I hear a man's voice.

"How long ago?" the deep voice asks.

It's Ranger Anderson.

"A little over a year ago now. Everything changed for Sadie that day." Mom's voice lowers to a near whisper.

I freeze.

"It's a hard thing to lose your father."

He knows. She must have told him even after promising she

wouldn't say anything to anyone. Dad died because of me, and now everyone will know.

I burst into the room, blood pumping, ready for a fight. I surprise Mom and Ranger Anderson, but that's not the only surprise. It's not just the two of them. Ronan is sitting on the floor with Rocky, whose left front paw looks newly bandaged. Ronan knows too.

"Oh." My response hangs in the air.

Mom was right when she said that everything changed for me that day. I no longer wanted to be me. I send Mom a cold look before running out of the room, through the clinic doors, and into the woods. It's the same path that I took the first day when I met Ronan and Rocky. I'm not able to get far before I need to rest. The events of the day catch up with me. I find a large log and feel the weight of my emotions pulling me down.

My phone beeps with a text. *I'm sorry you overheard that, Sadie. They know that Dad passed. They don't know the whole story. I love you.*

I turn off my phone and push it back into my bag. I sit on the log for a few minutes before I see Ronan coming my way. He doesn't say anything but sits down next to me. Silent tears begin to flow down my cheeks, and Ronan gently puts his arm around me, pulling me a little closer to him. The comfort I feel is unnerving but not unwelcome.

"Sadie, are you okay?" he asks in a soft voice.

You would think that I would be used to people asking me this, but it has been a long time since anyone asked. I don't think I've ever responded with anything other than a "yes" or an "I'm fine." But I'm not fine, and I haven't been for a long time. Pretending everything is okay all the time takes its toll, and at some point, it all becomes too much.

"No," I tell him, feeling for the first time that I'm being honest when answering that question.

"I'm sorry about your dad, Sadie."

I wipe my eyes and let out a shaky sigh.

"Do you want to talk about it?"

Yes. No. And everything between.

"Maybe one day."

Our eyes meet and whatever this is between us seems to grow deeper.

"Well, I hope one day you will." He holds out a hand and helps me up. Keeping our hands clasped, we walk back to the clinic without saying another word.

———

THE FALL FESTIVAL arrives as a school-wide celebration.

"I have to admit that while I have never actually been to a high school baseball game before, I'm pretty excited to see this game," I tell Anna on the phone.

"Okay, so tell me more about this Evan." I can practically see her settling onto her bed, ready for girl talk.

I sit on the window seat in my loft and look toward Ronan's house beyond the trees. "Evan has been really sweet, making sure I know everything going on at school and telling me so many stories about the past years that I almost feel like I had been there. It's hard not to be happy around Evan. With him and Gia, I never feel alone."

"I'm glad you're making friends." There's wistfulness in Anna's tone.

"I'm grateful for their friendships, but a part of me really needs some alone time too. When I'm feeling the need for space, I go to the animal sanctuary." The fresh air and presence of the animals works wonders for my mood, bringing about a peace that's hard to find elsewhere.

"I'm sure it's hard going anywhere after Great Bear." Anna is like me. We've never desired going to a big city or popular destination. We like the freedom the rainforest provides. "So, how's work going anyway? Anything new with Ronan?"

"I actually haven't seen Ronan at work recently. We're never scheduled for the same shift. At school the only class we have together is biology, and we barely talk. I've looked around for him during the breaks and lunch, but I never see him. I can't help but wonder if he's trying to avoid me."

This thought leaves me disappointed. Even though Ronan and I got off to a rough start, I find myself looking forward to spending time with him.

A text pops up on my phone. *On my way! Let's get this party started!"*

Even his texts are full of energy. I take a deep breath and try to summon the energy I need for tonight. I send back a thumbs up, but no more.

"Anna, I gotta go. Evan's on his way."

"Call me tonight?"

"As soon as I walk through the door."

Glancing in the vanity mirror, I give a little smile. I'm wearing a knee-length, red cotton sundress and freshly cleaned boots. When designing this one, I had embroidered white flowers down the length of the dress to add dimension and give it a casual yet feminine feel.

I pull my hair back into a long ponytail. A few curls fall around my face, and I tuck the longer strands behind my ears. I choose small, gold hoop earrings to go with my gold bear-paw necklace and rub a little Lavender essential oil onto my wrists and neck, the scent calming my nerves.

Taking a deep breath, I step away from the vanity. The weather forecast is perfect. A sunny seventy-five degrees during the day and only a little cooler in the evening. I open the windows in my loft. I find myself looking out these windows a lot. I haven't seen the man in the woods since that first night. But even though I haven't seen him, he crosses my mind most nights.

I move to the side window once again and look through the missing trees toward Ronan's cabin again. I have seen Ronan a few times outside his cabin this week. He's usually doing some kind of work, like chopping wood or removing broken tree branches. Today is different though. He's on the side of the cabin playing catch with a younger boy. I recognize him from the picture on Ronan's desk. It must be his brother, Declan. The boy looks to be around ten, and they are throwing a baseball around.

The familiar desire for a brother or sister returns. There were so many times growing up that I wished I wasn't an only child. Anna became like a sister to me, but as close as we are, it's not the same. There's a special bond between siblings that just exists. Declan throws the ball up high into the air as Ronan runs back and forth like it's the highest ball anyone has ever thrown, making Declan laugh. Ronan dives, catching the ball, and Declan jumps on him, trying to steal it away. A half-hearted wrestling match ensues, and I turn away from the window, reminding myself that Evan will be here any minute.

Grabbing my blue-jean jacket, I head down to the front porch to wait for him. At the sound of crunching rocks, I shake away any remaining thoughts of Ronan and focus on Evan as he pulls up in his red Jeep Rubicon.

"Nice Jeep!" He points to our white Wrangler.

I nod, suddenly at a loss for words.

He hops out of his Jeep and holds the door open for me. "You look great!"

"Thanks." I climb into the Jeep.

A pine-tree air freshener hangs from the rearview mirror. The scent is strong, not like the subtle scent of Ronan's truck. His back seat is covered with baseball gear, leaving no room for his friend.

"Is your friend still coming?"

"Oh, Teddy's getting a ride with Devon. We'll see them there." Evan shifts the gears and pulls down the driveway. "Have you thought anymore about playing in the game?"

Evan has been trying to get me to play in the game all week. I like baseball, and we used to play some in Great Bear. It's just that I want to watch today and avoid any attention. It hasn't been easy being the new girl at school. Sitting this out will hopefully take some of the attention off of me.

"I'm not going to play. Sorry." I see his look of disappointment. "But, maybe another time."

"I'm going to hold you to it."

Evan honks the horn twice as we pass Ronan's house. I look away, not wanting to see Ronan. Maybe being out with Evan is just what I need—a distraction from Ronan.

When we get to the school, the whole place has been transformed. There's a large, twinkling Ferris wheel, spinning rides, and game tents scattered around the grounds. Evan takes the baseball gear to the field with a few teammates, so I walk around, browsing the concession stands. Walking past a food stand, the smell of hotdogs and hamburgers almost stops me, but I decide to wait for Evan and go to the lemonade stand instead.

I'm deciding between a strawberry and peach lemonade when I see Ms. Maggie standing behind a long table of assorted pies. Festive leaves are draped delicately around the table, reminding me of the stationary Ms. Maggie makes. She cuts two large slices of apple pie for a little boy and his mom. I pay for my peach lemonade and walk her way.

As soon as she sees me, her eyes light up. "Sadie, so good to see you, dear! Come here and give Ms. Maggie a hug."

She wraps me in a hug like we haven't seen each other in years, instead of yesterday. Some of my lemonade spills, and I hold it as far away as I can.

"Hi, Ms. Maggie." I laugh. "These pies look amazing."

"If you think they look amazing, wait until you taste one. I'm just full of surprises." She winks at me as she unwraps more pies from their foil. The sun catches a piece of aluminum, sending the glare right at me and reminding me of the mystery man in the woods. Ms. Maggie knows everything that happens in Redwood Hills. Why have I not thought to ask her about the man?

"Ms. Maggie, do you know if there is anyone that patrols the woods at night around here?"

She hesitates for a moment before putting her manicured finger to her lips in a thoughtful gesture. "Patrolling the woods at night? Sometimes Ranger Anderson will be out checking on an animal. Why, dear? Did you see something?"

She leans in close, thirsty for any gossip I may share.

"The night we came here, I saw a man in the woods outside our cabin."

Her eyes narrow. "How do you know it was a man?"

"I don't know...It just looked like a man."

"Sounds like it might have been your mind playing tricks on you." She playfully points a finger at me.

I know she's just being Ms. Maggie, but it makes me feel silly for bringing it up. Could I have imagined it? It was a long drive, and I was tired and distracted.

"Maybe."

She gives me a sympathetic look. "There are times I swear I see Elvis himself. But that might just be wishful thinking on my part." She laughs with a far-off look in her eyes. It takes her a moment to come back. "Listen, if you think you see anyone else in the woods again, you give me a call, and I'll have it checked out. Sound good, love?"

A movement catches my eye. Ms. Hannon bumps into the table next to ours looking intently at a jar of grape jelly. She is close enough to have overheard our conversation.

I turn my back toward her and lean even closer to Ms. Maggie. "Yeah, I'll do that." I give her a hug. "Thanks, Ms. Maggie."

"Anytime. Now how about a piece of pie?" She waves her arm out across the table, and I laugh.

"I can't yet. I want to wait for Evan. He just went down to the field but should be back in a few minutes."

An odd expression crosses her face. "Evan Pawson is a good young man, a mighty fine baseball player, and..." Ms. Maggie pauses, like she wants to say more. Then she adds, "Oh, look at that. He's right behind you now."

"You're getting pie without me?" Evan feigns hurt. "I told you, Sadie, Ms. Maggie's pies are the best part of the whole festival."

"Now go on, the two of you." Ms. Maggie shoos us away with the pie slices.

"You're right. This is the best pie I have ever tasted." I take another bite.

"I know. She won't tell anyone her secret ingredient."

With full stomachs we walk to the baseball diamond. I join Gia on the bleachers while the players begin to warm up. There are a mix of baseball players, teachers, and people from the community, including Ronan's brother who was playing catch with him earlier. I learn from Gia that Evan and Ronan are both team captains for their respective teams, but they couldn't look more different leading workouts for their teams. Ronan is serious with his organized stretching and drills, while Evan is laughing and carrying on like he's hosting his own comedy show. But even with their very different styles, I can see how good they both are.

When the game is about to begin, Evan sends a big smile and two thumbs up my way. I wave back as the girls around us giggle.

"He's so cute," one girl whispers.

Gia rolls her eyes.

"You two are so cute together," Callie calls from two rows behind, a smirk twisted on her face.

I'm about to tell her that Evan and I are just friends, but she stands and waves to Ronan. "Good luck, babe! You've got this!"

The girls surrounding her cheer loudly, causing an uproar from the crowd. Evan coaxes the crowd on to cheer for his side, and the noise reaches a whole new level of loud. Before long the stands are thundering, but it quiets as soon as the home-plate umpire yells, "Play ball!"

I find myself completely immersed in the game. Home runs, amazing steals, and diving catches follow one after another. An argument erupts in the top of the sixth inning on an accused balk, and the two teams argue for much longer than necessary with every spectator having an opinion. It's finally decided by a pie eating contest between the pitcher and the batter, much to everyone's enjoyment. The pitcher finishes first, and the game continues without another mention of the play.

At the top of the ninth inning, the score is eight to seven, with Evan's home team leading. Bases are loaded, and there are two outs when Ronan comes up to bat. He has already had 2 doubles and a triple. The first pitch is a ball. The pitcher is very careful with each throw. The second is another ball, and the crowd begins booing.

"Give him something to hit," a man yells.

The third pitch is another ball, and the yelling intensifies.

The next pitch is hit hard to center field.

Both cheers and groans erupt as the ball seems to fly forever in the clear sky. The centerfielder jumps up on the outfield wall and reaches over as the ball falls. There's silence before the centerfielder hops off the fence, holding the ball in his glove. Another round of cheers vibrates the stands.

Evan's team runs out onto the field, hoisting the centerfielder up and chanting his name.

"Kev-in. Kev-in. Kev-in."

The two teams eventually line up and shake hands goodheartedly, and the crowd disperses. Callie and the other girls walk over to Ronan's dugout. I walk the opposite way with Gia toward the vendors when Ms. Hannon steps in front of us.

"Did you girls enjoy the game?"

"It was awesome! You're quite the hitter, Ms. Hannon!" Gia gives her a high five.

"Why thank you. I played a little softball in college." She does a funny curtsy.

"That's my sister." Gia points to a petite woman in her mid-twenties. She has the same shiny, dark hair as Gia, but it's cut into a straight bob. She's holding a toddler in her arms. "I need to check in with her, but I'll catch up with you in a bit, Sadie. See you Ms. Hannon."

I look to the ground, unsure about standing alone with a teacher.

"How are you doing with the move? I know moving is never easy." There's a kindness in her voice that makes me relax a little.

"Okay. I really like it here. It's just a lot to get used to, you know?"

"I do." She smiles. "Remember, I'm new around here too. It takes a little to get used to everything. The research center has really helped me though."

"The gardens look great. I know everyone really appreciates your volunteer work."

Ms. Hannon has been spending some afternoons each week at the center, mostly working in the flower garden. With her background in botany, it is the perfect job for her.

"Oh. Well gardening has always been a hobby of mine." She looks around us and then leans in. "Listen, I accidentally overheard you tell Ms. Maggie about a man you saw in the woods. Could you describe what you saw?"

"Why?" Goosebumps prickle my neck.

"It's just I thought I saw someone in the woods by my place too. I thought it was nothing, but then when I heard you did too, it just made me wonder." There's a neediness in her eyes.

"There you are!" Evan wraps his arms around me and swings me in a circle, causing a nervous laugh to escape my lips.

Disappointment swims in Ms. Hannon's eyes. "Well, you two have a great night." She quickly walks away.

While I'm relieved at Evan's interruption, I'm also a little disappointed. I want to believe Ms. Maggie and assume it was just an illusion, but something in Ms. Hannon's tone tells me that she knows more than she's letting on. But the question is - what does she know?

CHAPTER SIX

Fireflies light up the sky as evening descends on the Fall Festival. Evan and I join a group setting up blankets on the main field. I've been trying to put everything out of my mind and focus on my time with him, but the conversations between Ms. Maggie and Ms. Hannon are replaying in the back of my mind. It's taking all of my effort be present.

The thought doesn't last long as Gia waves us over to join her and Ronan. When we join them, Evan takes my hand and Ronan's eyes darken. Shifting on my feet, I look away and help spread out our blanket.

Evan nudges me with his elbow. "Ferris wheel? We should have just enough time before the fireworks."

"Sure," I reply with a little too much enthusiasm.

As we get in line for the Ferris wheel, Evan takes my hand. I feel someone approach—not just someone, but Ronan. He's standing there with a little girl who resembles the girl from the photo on his desk.

I drop Evan's hand before I know what I'm doing. Luckily a guy from the baseball team comes over to rehash the game, so he doesn't seem to notice.

"Hi, I'm Maeve. You're really pretty, like Rapunzel," the little girl says.

She has her brother's caramel eyes. Her auburn hair is pulled into two low braids with blue ribbons at the ends. She has a soft, rounded face and looks adorable in her baby-blue cotton dress with white sandals and a thin, white jacket with a unicorn on the pocket. Her little hand is protectively curled in her big brother's.

"Hi, Maeve." I smile back at her. "Thank you. That's so sweet. You are so beautiful, just like Belle."

She beams at this.

"I'm Sadie." I bend down to shake her hand.

Her eyes widen with recognition. "Sadie! My brother told us all about you."

Ronan bites his lip and tugs gently on one of her braids.

"Oh, did he?" Please tell me more.

"Yes, he said he's never met anyone like you. And that you're working at the animal sanctuary. And that you're really pretty."

Ronan looks around as though he's looking for an escape route.

Sensing that what she said was a big deal, Maeve continues like only children can when they have someone's undivided attention. "Yeah, I always ask Ronan if a girl is pretty, but he just says 'yeah.'" She shrugs imitating her brother with amazing precision. "But when I asked him about you, he got all red and said that you're the prettiest girl he's ever met."

Maeve holds her head high, standing there with a big smile on her face, which matches my smile. Ronan's face flushes as he looks up into the sky.

The Ferris wheel grinds to a stop, and the line begins moving. Evan grabs my hand again, and we climb into the seat. The ride operator locks the swinging door, and we begin to rock back and forth as the next chair takes our place. I catch Ronan's eyes, and he gives me a pained smile before getting into the seat with his sister. Maeve waves to me, and I wave back.

Suddenly I'm very happy to have met Ronan's little sister.

THE NEXT FEW weeks of school pass quickly. I've settled into a rhythm during the school day. Since I normally drive my mom to the research center before school, I have some freedom in the morning before my first class. Sometimes I'll meet up with Gia before class, but more often, I find myself in the art room working on my textiles project. Today it's nice to spend a Saturday morning in the cabin. It's the first one when I'm not scheduled at the sanctuary, and I'm taking advantage of the quiet while Mom is at work.

I really need this time because my emotions have been all over the place recently. Things with Evan are good, but as much as I was hoping he would be the distraction I needed from Ronan, the connection is just not there. He's becoming a good friend, and his upbeat energy is contagious, which I've needed since thoughts of Ronan are leaving me more and more confused.

Ronan hasn't mentioned anything about what Maeve said that night. We will talk briefly in passing at school or at the sanctuary, but he seems to be keeping his distance. I have noticed him looking my way at times in biology though, and those quick moments give my heart hope. I pick up my teacup and swirl the herbal tea before taking a generous sip. The soothing aroma and warmth fill my senses, and thoughts of Ronan begin to drift away.

I curl my legs up on the wooden Adirondack chair. I need a distraction, and being outside has always brought me peace. There's a small garden behind our cabin. The previous vet enjoyed gardening, and his work is immaculate. The vegetable beds have removable chicken wire covers to protect them from curious forest animals. The root bed contains a mixture of carrots, beets, and onions while the green bed contains lettuce, chard, and spinach. Another bed is perpendicular to the first two, creating a T-shaped design with little stone walkways between them. The third bed contains tomatoes, cucumbers, and broccoli. I lean over and snap off a leaf from the mint plant for my tea.

While Mom loves tending to the vegetables, I enjoy the flower beds. The lavender, another member of the mint family, is my favorite for both scent and design. I often use flowers as a guide for my clothing. I try to incorporate the shapes and textures of nature into the design of my piece. I'm inspired by the softness of the petals and the symmetry of the leaves. My style is different from the style of other girls in Redwood Hills. Sometimes I see them looking at one of my dresses or my boots, and it makes me feel like I'm under scrutiny. But I'm not sure what the verdict is.

After lunch I drive through the back roads of Redwood Hills, stopping at the sight of Roosevelt elk grazing on meadow grass in a clearing. It's an incredible sight to see. The males are huge, probably weighing in close to one thousand pounds. Their antlers are a piece of art, so perfectly designed, branching out like extensive branches of a magnificent tree. It's a wonder how they can even hold their heads up, but they do so with a sense of royalty that only one with complete comfort in itself can manage.

Could I ever embrace myself, my whole self, just as I am? It's a question I don't want to try to answer right now, so I start the engine instead. When I arrive at the research center, Mom is still finishing with a client, so I wait in her office. I never told her about the dreams. I've decided to just try to put them out of my mind. Although I'm not having much success with that.

Rocky whines from his spot by my feet, staring longingly at the door. When I walked in on Mom's conversation with Ranger Anderson and Ronan, she had been treating Rocky for bites on his leg from a long-tailed weasel. It turns out Rocky tends not only to run off after people but also animals, and the weasel was his latest encounter. He's under Mom's orders to stay out of trouble and keep the wounds clean, so he's been spending a lot of time indoors this week while Ronan works. I can't imagine being cooped up for so long.

"Wanna go for a walk?" I ask conspiratorially.

He jumps up and begins dancing in a circle smacking his tail on everything within reach. I wrestle him into a hug to hook on his leash. We walk around the clinic, and he stops about every two feet to smell or mark something.

"Come on, Rocky." I pull him, but instead of following me, he starts digging by the base of the statue. This won't go over well with Mom.

"Stop it!" I tug on his leash, but it only causes him to dig harder until he suddenly stops, his tail wagging proudly.

A thin, red wire peeks out from the remaining dirt. Reaching down, I give it a gentle pull. Whether from me or Rocky, it's now disconnected on one end, exposing the sharp, silver connector. It looks familiar, and I scour my memory until finally placing it.

A few years ago, Dad used a wire just like this to set up a security camera in Great Bear. There had been a few attempts to break the lock on the research base, and the research team set up a camera system to try to catch whoever was trying to break in. We never saw anyone on the videos, and there weren't any more attempted break-ins, so it was eventually forgotten. But I remember this cable because my job was to hold the end while they worked.

I look around for the source of the wire, but I don't see any cameras. Maybe it is old and was never removed? No. Wouldn't Ms. Hannon have seen it when she was raking the flower bed? It doesn't make sense. Unless...I kneel down beside the statue, running my hand across the smooth surface. A sharp edge by the rabbit's mouth scrapes the palm of my hand. A thin line of blood appears. The bunny's nose hides the opening of the mouth, and I lean in closer to get a better look. In the little opening is a tiny, circular lens of a camera.

Who would put a hidden camera here? It's not even pointed toward the base but rather looks out into the surrounding woods. Before my mind can run away with all kinds of crazy ideas, I remind myself that it's completely normal to have a hidden security camera at the research center. We did at Great Bear. It would be weirder not to have one. I've almost convinced myself but can't resolve the fact that this area and the statue were Ms. Hannon's project.

Glancing around to make sure no one is watching, I drop the wire back in the hole and cover it with dirt. Whoever put it there will find out soon enough that it's been disconnected, and I wonder how long it will be before someone questions me about it. The camera must have captured me and Rocky walking over to it, and now I'm wishing we stayed in Mom's office.

Instead of going back, we walk to the nearest trail. Rocky whines and pulls harder on the leash. He must be used to walking this trail, and it would be good for him to do something normal. Good for me too. The sun is just beginning to set, so we have a little time to walk the first part of the trail before it gets too dark.

As soon as we step foot on the trail, I instantly feel better. Rocky prances along the path.

"Okay, now don't get any dirtier, or we'll both be in trouble."

We walk for about fifteen minutes before turning around, and that's when I realize that at some point, we went off the main trail. There are no markers in sight, and it's getting darker and harder to see our surroundings. We only make it a few feet toward what I hope is the way back when Rocky goes still, ears and tail alert.

"What is it, boy?" I gently stroke his head.

He doesn't respond but just continues to stare into the distance. His hair raises on his back, and a low growl murmurs in his throat. I try to pull him forward, but he won't budge. Feeling desperate now, I beg him to start walking while keeping my eyes on the woods before us. There's stillness in the air now. Rocky's growls are the only sound.

And then I see it.

Crouched behind a patch of redwood sorrel is a large, tan mountain lion. It's crouched down, hind legs bent, ready to pounce. Its mouth hangs slightly open, revealing sharp, yellow teeth. We're close enough to see the green rings of its eyes, which don't blink but stare intently at us—just like prey. A chill runs down my spine as I realize that's just what we are.

Then I remember Fluffy. Since we've been in Redwood Hills, I've heard Ms. Maggie tell the mountain lion story at least five times. She always says how she scared the large cat away by raising her arms and making a lot of noise. I've seen the sign at the sanctuary instructing people to never run, so I know that's not an option. But I also know that the mountain lion is most likely more interested in Rocky than me. What would I do if something happens to Rocky because of me? If another life is lost because of my weakness, I don't know how I'll survive.

My whole-body pulses in union with my heartbeat. Its rhythm echoes in my ears. I raise my arms, and the cat follows the movement with its eyes. But while doing so, I unknowingly loosen my grip on Rocky's leash. He pulls forward a few more steps, and the lion hisses revealing more teeth as it arches its back. I yell as loudly as I can. Rocky immediately answers with growling and snapping. The lion lowers its head, and I close my eyes not wanting to see what's coming next.

A loud horn sounds, and I open my eyes in time to see the lion running off into the thicket. I turn around and watch Dr. Allen, dressed in hiking gear, walking toward us.

"Are you okay?" He fumbles to close the zipper on his backpack, and the horn falls to the ground. I pick it up and hand it to him. He immediately tucks it into the outside pocket of his bag.

"Thank you," I say in a voice that sounds calmer than I actually feel. My eyes rest on his bag, and he jerks it onto his back, sharply snapping the strap hook across his chest. He keeps his free hand over the clasp.

The sound of footsteps breaks the tense silence. Mom, Ranger Anderson, and Ronan push through the bushes. Even in the dim light I can see the worry etched on Mom's face, and the guilt hits hard. What was I thinking coming out here with Rocky?

"What happened?" she asks, trying to catch her breath.

"Everything's fine," I say calmly. "I was just taking Rocky for a quick walk, and we kind of, well, ran into a mountain lion."

The remaining color drains from her face.

"But Dr. Allen blew the horn and scared it away."

The look of appreciation and gratitude Mom gives Dr. Allen immediately makes me regret saying it.

Mom hugs me. "What were you thinking?"

Her tone irks me. "Everything is fine."

She narrows her eyes. "Sadie, it is not fine to walk off into the woods without telling anyone. It is dangerous. And to take Rocky when you know his condition. You both could have been killed."

"It's always my fault, isn't it Mom?"

We stare at each other, and silent pain comes between us.

"We should start walking back before it gets darker," Ranger Anderson interjects, for which I'm grateful.

Ronan walks next to me as we follow Mom and Dr. Allen. Ranger Anderson follows a few steps behind us, still surveying the woods.

Ronan reaches over and takes Rocky's leash without saying a word. His jaw is clenched, and his expression is stone cold.

"I'm sorry, Ronan." I fidget with my hands. "I never wanted to put Rocky in danger. I had no idea that mountain lion was there."

Ronan gives me a sharp look. "Sadie, I'm glad Rocky was with you. He would have protected you, or at the very least distracted the lion from you. If he hadn't been there..." His voice trails off.

We continue in silence, and our footsteps become the only sound. The air is so tense it's unbearable by the time we reach the research center.

"I remembered Fluffy and what Ms. Maggie had said," I blurt out to no one in particular. "I felt like Ms. Maggie was there with me when we saw the mountain lion." My voice is a pitch too high.

There is a low murmur of what I guess could be considered laughter, but not the effect I was hoping for.

"Sadie, you had a close call," Ranger Anderson says seriously. "That lion was most likely Sienna."

His mouth forms a tense line. "Her den is only a few hundred yards away from where you were. Her kittens are about four months old now, and she's very protective of them. She could attack without much provocation."

When I look at Ronan, I know he's well-aware of this. "Mountain lions attack by leaping right for the neck or head. They are fast and strong, and a mother will do anything to protect her young."

"I guess we're lucky that Dr. Allen was close by then," Mom says, sending another grateful look to Dr. Allen.

Ranger Anderson looks away but gives a single nod. "Yes, it's lucky you happened to be there." He shoots a dangerous glare in Dr. Allen's direction before turning away and heading into the lodge.

Mom goes to close the clinic while the rest of us update Ms. Maggie about the incident. She records our story in a large binder on her desk. I try my best to get a glimpse into the binder, but Ms. Maggie slams it shut and slides it into a drawer under her desk. She locks the drawer with a small key before tucking it away in her bag. "Well, Colin darling, there's an issue with that fence by the sanctuary again. Why don't we go see what can be done?"

They leave together, with Ms. Maggie's bag securely tucked under her arm. My mind is running through any possible excuse I can come up with to go with them, but I draw a blank and lose sight of them in the darkness.

"Well, I better get going," Dr. Allen announces with slight hesitation in his voice. He's also looking out the window in the direction they went. "But you kids have fun tomorrow." He hurries out the door in the same direction as Ranger Anderson and Ms. Maggie.

"Tomorrow?" I ask absently.

"Homecoming."

The softness in Ronan's voice pulls my attention away from the window and from whatever is going on outside.

"Oh. Right."

"So..." He shifts his feet. "Are you going with Evan?"

"No. We're just friends."

Well, that came out a little more forceful than I meant, but there's a brightness in his eyes that wasn't there a moment ago.

"Are you going?" Now it's my turn to shift nervously, unsure if I really want to know the answer.

"Yeah."

The word is like a brick, and my heart sinks.

"But just with a group of friends."

And just like that the brick falls away, and my heart leaps.

"Same here. Gia says it's the best way to go."

"She has a point, but I'm not sure it's the best way to go."

His comment makes me wonder what it would be like to go to homecoming with Ronan.

"I better get Rocky home," he says, patting Rocky's big head. "I'll see you tomorrow."

As he walks out of the door, thoughts of mountain lions and mysterious men in the woods are replaced by his warm caramel eyes and images of dancing under the stars.

CHAPTER SEVEN

I spend the afternoon before the homecoming dance working on my textiles project. I sew knots into the fabric, creating various depths to the images. My cell phone rings a few times, and I glance at the screen.

"Hey, Anna."

"Ah, it's so good to hear your voice."

"Same here. How is everything?"

"Okay. Jason is busy preparing for university." There's a sadness in her voice.

Anna and Jason have always been close. He just turned eighteen and was accepted on a full scholarship into the two-year Fisheries and Aquaculture Technology program at Canada Research University. Jason has always loved the water, and he will have the chance to work with Fisheries and Oceans Canada, spending more than a quarter of his training in the field. It sounds incredible and not an opportunity to be taken lightly.

"I know it will be hard without him."

"Everyone is hoping he will return to Great Bear to work with the rest of the research team. I can picture Jason on the team."

I know it has always been Papa Jay's hope. "That would be great. I know how hard it is to leave Great Bear. I can image that he will want to return."

She clears her throat. "Tell me more about Ronan and this home-coming dance."

"Well, first, I'm not going with Ronan. We're both just going with a group of friends. Second, I honestly don't know what's going on with Ronan."

"Is it like with Jason? Are you following him around and sketching pictures of him in your notebook? Man, you know, now that I think about it, that was kind of creepy." She laughs, reminding me of my embarrassing childhood crush on her brother.

"It kind of was," I agree, "but no, this is not like that at all. I don't know. I can't explain it. He's so good with the animals and really cares about the sanctuary. He's strong but incredibly gentle. When we're together there is this thing between us. When he looks at me, it's like he really sees me."

It's not until the words are out of my mouth that I understand it to be true. I finally have put words to the way I'm feeling about Ronan.

"Wow. So does he have a twin?"

I laugh, missing Anna so much.

"Seriously, I can't wait to meet him."

The thought of Anna coming here and meeting Ronan is surreal, like two worlds colliding.

"Do you think you'll be able to visit soon?"

"Well, Mama Rose thinks in the springtime."

Months away.

"That would be great." I try to hide my disappointment.

"What are you wearing to the dance tonight?"

"My rose satin dress."

"Oh, love that one! It looks so good on you!"

Last year, Mama Rose found the most beautiful fabric on a trip to Vancouver. I designed a long flowing dress with rose and vine-like embellishments down the length. I made a sweetheart neckline that lays smooth along my skin. It's one of the dresses I'm most proud of creating. Mama Rose and I made it special for this banquet the research team was invited to in Anchorage, Alaska. There were scientists from all over the world, most of which study bears in one location or another. While my parents attended a few banquets in the past, this was the first time that Anna and I were allowed to go. And it was the first one where my dad wasn't there.

It was held at this beautiful hotel in Anchorage, in the most elegant ballroom. There were large windows looking out to crystallized water that seemed to come from a dream. I watched as the seaplanes came in and out. Anna was enthralled because she has wanted to fly her own plane since we were little. As she continued to watch the planes, I looked around at the people all dressed in gorgeous dresses and black suits. The food and drinks were arranged on the long tables draped in white tablecloth. A three-person band was on one side with a dance floor, and people were coupling up to dance.

It was my first chance to dance. I mean, Anna and I would dance around to our favorite songs, but never at an actual dance or with a boy. There was a boy that night. Lucas was there with his dad, a biologist studying the Eurasian brown bear. A couple years older than me and from Sweden, he told me about his plans to study Environmental Engineering at a university in California. When he asked me to dance, I felt like I was in a fairy tale. But we only danced for the first few notes before it all ended.

The band was playing "Wonderful Tonight"—my parents' song. I remembered watching them dance to the song every year on their anniversary. I apologized to Lucas and told him I would be back. When I found Mom, I could tell she was trying to hold it together, but she was breaking down inside. So I went with her out into the hallway to get away from the music. Almost immediately she said she was tired and needed to get back to our room. I had no choice but to go with her. I couldn't leave her alone. These moments come in waves for Mom. I think her heart died a little the day Dad died.

When I finally made it back to the ballroom that night, Lucas was already gone. Looking at my phone, I realized that I had been with Mom for almost an hour, and the banquet was about to end. I never had my first dance.

"Sadie, you there?" Anna asks with concern edging her voice.

"Yeah, sorry. I was just thinking."

The silence lets me know that Anna has followed my trail of thoughts. A beep sounds on my phone as Gia's text message comes through.

"I'm on my way!"

"Hey Anna, I have to go. Gia is on her way over. We're getting ready for homecoming together."

"Sure." The disappointment is obvious in her tone. "Send me pictures! I want to see everything."

We end our call, and I promise to send her photos and an update later tonight. I pull my dress and the gold-colored flats out of my closet. Maybe tonight I'll finally have my first dance.

ALL MY HOPES of a fairy-tale dance seem to vanish within the first five minutes of the dance. I take my punch cup and make my way to the side bleachers of the gym. The punch is a bright, unnatural color of red and tastes like pure sugar. I only take one sip before tossing it into the trash. I watch Gia laughing on the dance floor with Travis. Her short, black dress and high ponytail sway with the beat of the music.

I'm about to rub my tired eyes, but remember Gia insisted on doing my makeup, including my darkened, smokey eyes. I use the napkin from my punch to gently wipe some of the heavy eye shadow off, leaving only a smudge of color, mascara, and a deep rose color on my lips. I'm thankful that I didn't let Gia pull my hair back and instead left it down in long, loose curls, providing a curtain to hide behind.

I'm twirling a strand of hair when Ronan walks through the door. My instant excitement fades when Callie steps in behind him. She looks incredible. Her short black hair is pinned up into a twist on the top of her head, with pieces of shiny strands framing her face. Her short, red dress and red lipstick creates a sophisticated look—one I know I could never pull off. She puts her hand on Ronan's shoulder while whispering something in his ear, and he laughs.

Jealousy hits me in a flash as I can't help but acknowledge how incredible they look together. Dressed in a black button-down shirt and olive-green khakis, Ronan looks so handsome.

I have to get out of here.

I'm deciding on the best exit route when our eyes meet, and he walks my way. The bleacher moves with his weight as he sits beside me.

"Hey."

With one word, everything seems to fade away around us, and it's just me and him. And man, he looks even better up close.

"It's kind of a loud mess, huh?" Ronan's dark hair falls over his forehead as he turns to me.

"Yeah. I guess dances aren't really my thing either."

Ronan laughs, and there goes my heart.

"I was actually just thinking about leaving."

"Come on. Give it a chance. Five minutes, okay?" His eyes hold mine. There's a subtle plead there that I can't resist.

"I can do five minutes."

We talk about everything from our favorite ice cream flavors to music and books. By the time a lull in our conversation settles, almost two hours have passed. The quiet between us isn't awkward but rather like that of old friends.

A loud dance song blares from the speakers and Ronan moves closer to me. "What was it like growing up in Great Bear?"

He's so close that our arms are touching. His warmth is so distracting that it takes me a moment to answer. "Amazing."

He looks at me with his full attention, urging me to continue.

"I grew up in the forest, running through the trees and playing in the water. I always felt so free. The forest has always been home to me."

"Sounds amazing. I know what you mean about the forest. There's nowhere else I'd rather be."

"You've never wanted to live anywhere besides Redwood Hills?"

He shakes his head. "Never. There are moments when the small-town life frustrates me, but I've never wanted to leave."

"I understand that. At times it's hard being so far from Great Bear."

"Do you think you'll ever feel like Redwood Hills is your home?" There's a mixture of hope and hesitation in his eyes.

"I don't know. I hope so."

"I hope so too."

Gia sends me a thumbs up, and I try to wave her off before Ronan notices. The curve of his mouth suggests I was too late.

"I didn't realize Dr. Allen is chaperoning."

I follow Ronan's gaze to the corner of the room. Dr. Allen is standing against the wall and sipping from a paper cup. He's scanning the room and stops at us. He waves, nearly spilling his cup.

"Me neither."

Ms. Hannon joins him, but he immediately begins to walk a loop around the perimeter. Just the thought of him watching us makes my skin crawl. I look to the dance floor and catch Callie casting a murderous look our way.

"What's wrong?" Ronan nudges me with his knee.

I trace the rosebud embroidery on my dress, looking for answers to questions I can't yet put together. "Nothing. It's just people always seem to be looking at me. I know I'm the new girl and all, but it's a lot, you know?"

"I don't really think people look at you just because you're new. I think people look at you because you're beautiful. I mean, how could they not look at you?"

My heart soars straight out of my chest. There's a vulnerability I haven't seen before in his features. Hearing it from his sister was one thing but hearing Ronan express his feelings to me is another experience altogether. He looks at me in a way that makes me feel like I'm the only person in the room. His eyes drift to my lips, and I wonder if he's going to kiss me. A flutter of nerves flies through me.

The auditorium lights blink twice, interrupting the moment.

Ronan clears his throat. "That's their way of saying get out—the dance is over. Five more minutes, and then they'll turn the lights on and push everyone out like cattle."

I silently curse those lights.

Gia waves to me from across the dance floor and points to the door. "Gia's my ride, and it looks like we're leaving." I stand up. "But I'm glad I gave it five minutes. Maybe dances are my thing after all."

He laughs, which is quickly becoming one of my favorite sounds in the world. We've come so far since that first day in the woods. "Yeah, well next time, save a dance for me, okay? Or, at least a spot on the bleachers."

I can't imagine it any other way. Maybe the next time I will finally have my first dance.

As I follow Gia out the door, I turn around once more. Our eyes meet and his mouth curves up in that adorable smile. I would bet anything that smile will be in my dreams tonight.

———

ON OUR WAY out of the dance, we run into Dr. Allen. The visitor's name tag hangs on his crisp, white button-down shirt.

"You girls look beautiful," he says, grinning like a bobcat.

I wrap my arms around myself so tightly my shoulders ache. Gia, on the other hand, just gives him a playful push.

"Oh, Uncle Eric. Hope it wasn't too boring for you in there."

"Oh no. It was a delightful time. Having the chance to see you all dancing and having so much fun. Young love never ceases to amaze me." He sends me a pointed look, and the back of my neck prickles. He was watching me and Ronan.

Gia sighs dramatically. "Well, I don't know about love, but it was fun. Right, Sadie?"

"Yeah." I force the word out of my mouth. Dr. Allen looks at me like I'm a puzzle he's trying to put together. I take a step away and inadvertently bump into Ms. Hannon.

"Oh, Sadie, are you okay?" She grabs my arm to keep me from falling.

"Yeah, sorry." I straighten myself, feeling uncoordinated and distracted.

She glances me over before turning to Dr. Allen. "I was hoping to have a chance to speak with you during the dance, but you were always occupied."

"It's always a pleasure to speak with you, Ms. Hannon. I do hope you're enjoying your time at the research center. I seem to see you more inside than in the gardens. If there's ever anything you need help finding, just let me know, and I'd be happy to help you out." His cool tone contradicts his words.

"That would be wonderful. Thank you. I appreciate you taking such an interest in me." Ms. Hannon smiles back a little too sweetly.

The two of them appraise each other in a way that reminds me of the intense poker games the research team would play during those long winter nights in Great Bear, staring each other down and trying to find a weakness in their bluffs.

"I don't mean to interrupt, but Sadie and I need to get going. We don't want to be seen talking with the chaperones all night," Gia jokes, giving them each a side hug before pulling me along after her.

"Wait, Gia!" Dr. Allen calls. "I told your sister that I would give you girls a ride home. It only makes sense since I'm already here."

I try to come up with any excuse not to ride to Gia's house with him but come up empty. Ms. Hannon watches me intently. Her lips form a tight line.

"We're riding in your car? Sadie, just wait to you see his car, ah!" Gia is as thrilled by this change of plans as I am distressed.

"Well, Ms. Hannon, I hope we can speak sometime soon," Dr. Allen says with a dismissive nod before turning toward the parking lot, with me and Gia following behind. Gia is practically skipping, and my feet are dragging like two-ton weights are tied to my ankles. I look behind us, and Ms. Hannon stands unmoving, arms crossed over her chest.

When we reach Dr. Allen's car, I'm surprised to see a sleek, black Mercedes-Benz Coupe. It looks very expensive.

"Isn't it incredible?" Gia asks me.

"Yeah, it's g-great," I stammer.

"Come on, climb in." She ducks into the back and waves for me to follow.

As we drive away, I notice a dark car parked on the edge of the parking lot, just out of sight of the lights. Why would a car be parked over there?

Dr. Allen revs up the engine and pulls forward, but not before I get a glimpse of the bright, white hair through the driver's side window.

We speed out of the parking lot, and I grab onto the handle on the door, my knuckles turning white from the pressure.

"He has a bit of a heavy foot." Gia giggles.

That's the understatement of the century. "Seriously, how fast is he going?" I whisper and try to get a look at the speedometer on the dashboard.

AC/DC's "You Shook Me All Night Long" blares out the windows. Gia bobs along with the music as the wind whips around us. Dr. Allen begins singing along. His voice screeches at every high note.

After what feels like forever, he makes a sharp turn onto a side street. He lowers the music, and his hands go back to the ten-and-two position on the wheel. He's the model of a perfect chaperone, driving just below the speed limit. He gently pulls up in front of a log cabin with bright, yellow shutters and children's toys scattered in the front yard.

"Thanks for the ride, Uncle Eric. See you soon!" Gia climbs out and searches her purse for the key to the cabin.

I reach for the door handle, but Dr. Allen is already holding the outside handle, and it won't budge.

"Please, allow me." He slowly opens the door and reaches for my hand.

"I'm good." I brush his hand away.

"You look just like your mom when we were younger."

I rush past him and follow Gia to the door. I hold my breath as she unlocks the door, and I nearly push my way inside.

Is the door enough to keep him away?

When we get upstairs to Gia's room, she can't stop talking about the dance and boys while my memories are revolving between the awkward conversation with Dr. Allen and Ms. Hannon and the terrifying car ride home. All I want to remember is Ronan, but the way Dr. Allen was looking at me keeps coming back instead. It was as though he wasn't seeing me but rather Mom.

The look on Ms. Hannon's face when we were leaving was like a warning. Her interaction with Dr. Allen was odd. There's something weird about Ms. Hannon, and I can't put my finger on it. It's like she's keeping some kind of secret and trying hard to cover it up. And most of the time it works, but then there are times, like tonight, where I see glimpses of another side of her.

"Sadie, are you listening to me?" Gia raises her eyebrows pointedly.

"Oh, sorry. I'm just a little distracted."

"I bet you are," she teases. "I could feel the heat between you and Ronan all the way across the dance floor. You guys were intense."

When I don't say anything, she shakes her head. "Okay, let's go to bed, but I want all the details tomorrow."

Maybe tomorrow will bring some answers.

CHAPTER EIGHT

The next day Ronan and I are scheduled to do the evening feeding at the sanctuary. These evenings are quickly becoming my favorite time at work. There's something about the quiet and the routine of the chores that refreshes me after a long day.

I step into my long, navy cotton skirt and pull on a white Redwood Hills Animal Sanctuary T-shirt, knotting it on the side of my hip. Looking in the mirror, I see a flush on my cheeks. I look alive for the first time in months.

Thunder rumbles outside my window as dark clouds roll in from the west. I look into the woods like I do so often, trying to see if the man is lurking somewhere in the shadows. I haven't seen any signs of him since that first night. The trees sway from the incoming wind, causing shadows to dance around. Even if someone is there, it would be hard to tell now. I close the shutters and make my way downstairs.

Mom sits at the kitchen table, files strewn across the surface.

I pick up the car keys from the counter. "I'm leaving for work."

"Okay," she murmurs.

I slide past her and grab my green rain jacket from the closet. When I reach the front door, Mom calls to me.

"Wait!" She pushes her reading glasses up on her head. "How was homecoming last night?"

She finally remembered.

"It was fine."

"Did you dance with anyone?" She folds her hands in her lap and looks at me expectantly.

"No." She doesn't hide her disappointment.

"I gotta go. Bye, Mom." I close the door and hurry to the Jeep, needing the peace I know the sanctuary will bring.

WHEN I ARRIVE at the sanctuary, I go straight to the stables to start prepping for the evening treatments. The horses crowd around the pasture gate while I pour grain into the buckets. Cosmo is in the back of the herd, standing just outside of their circle. His blue eyes stand out even from a distance. He takes a few steps closer when he catches sight of me, but then stops. A brown Quarter Horse walks toward him with ears pinned back, and Cosmo trots farther away. Herd dynamics are an intricate balance of strength and leadership. I am so immersed in studying the horses' interactions that I don't hear Ronan come up behind me.

"I was just talking to Colin," he says, following my gaze. "Cosmo's court case is officially closed. He is now legally a member of Redwood Hills. So, it looks like you'll be seeing a lot more of him."

The news is so unexpected that I give a little screech and hug Ronan, catching him off guard. He quickly rights himself though and puts his arms around me, hugging me back. "That's amazing. I can't believe it all worked out so quickly."

"Yeah, Colin said his owners have had abuse and neglect charges in the past, so it made things easier to prove before the judge. They should never be able to hurt another animal ever again."

Ronan and I finish the feeding and treatments together, and I spend a few extra minutes with Cosmo, stroking his strong neck.

The sky has grown so dark that it's hard to see much in the dim moonlight. The outdoor lights flicker as thunder rumbles around us. A sizzling sound fills the air, and the lights flicker once more before going dark. With only the moon as a guide, heavy raindrops begin to fall, and I run back toward the barn's office door. Grabbing the handle, I pull but the door won't open. Ronan runs up behind me and gives it a hard tug, but it's no use. We're locked out.

"The door must've locked when the electricity went out." He tries the handle once more. The metal awning above us is chiming with the sound of the rain—a soothing melody that seems to be playing just for us. "The generator should come on soon. So, we won't be stuck for too long."

I realize that Ronan's trying to make me feel better. He's always taking care of everyone. The animals, his family, and now me. I've been taking care of myself for so long that there's relief in letting go.

I clear my throat. "You think the horses are okay?" We watch as the horses eat their hay under the field shelter with not a care in the world.

"I think they're okay." I hear the smile in his voice.

I playfully elbow his arm but then jump out of the way as water drips through the awning forming puddles around us.

"Come with me." Ronan grabs my hand, and we run around the side of the building to a run-in shed. Since the run-in is only open on one side, the grass toward the back is only slightly damp. Ronan takes a blanket from a hook in the far corner and lays it on the grass, its blue Gingham pattern inviting us to sit. "We can stay here and wait out the storm."

We settle onto the blanket and stare out into the darkness. From the opening we can see up into the dark clouds, the stars creating a hazy gleam throughout the sky.

"I used to come here a lot," he tells me, seriousness in his voice. "I guess you could say it was my escape." The same vulnerability that I saw last night is back in his eyes.

"We all need an escape sometimes." That's a truth I'm currently living.

"True. But sometimes people escape and never come back, like my dad."

I turn to him. "What happened with your dad?"

"I wish I could say that I'm sorry he left, but I can't. I hate him for what he did. He was always an arrogant, self-centered man. Always caring more about appearances than being with us. Whenever he was around, everything was always about him. Not my brother or sister, and definitely not my mom."

"That sounds awful."

He looks down and pulls the edge of the blanket closer to us, so the mud doesn't run on it. "Most nights he would come home drunk, slamming doors and yelling. When I was little, I would lay in my bed and count down until it was finally quiet when he finally passed out. As I got older though, I did everything I could to make sure everything was just how he liked it so there would be no yelling. I wanted to keep my brothers and sister safe. I would lay awake all night wishing he was dead and out of our lives. I vowed to myself that I would never drink. That I would never be like him."

I can't imagine what Ronan had to go through. To wish your father was dead is a horrible way to live. My father's death changed everything for me and Mom. What I wouldn't give for him to be back with us. To harbor that much resentment must be hard to overcome.

"Ronan, you're nothing like him."

"I always worry that it will be one thing that will push me over, just like him. People tell me that he had a sickness. I mean, I guess that's what addiction is."

"Did he get treatment?" I ask.

Ronan scoffs. "Yup."

"It didn't help?"

"It helped him." Bitterness drips from each word.

"And that wasn't good?"

"Not for us. My mom received the bills from the rehab each month. She was happy to pay them, thinking he was going to get better and come home afterward. She wanted to be a family again." He pauses. "But he didn't come back. After his treatment, he started a new life with a woman he met in the rehab. He told my mom that this was his chance to start over, to have a chance at a new life. She was waiting for him to come home and begin a new life with us, but he said he couldn't come back. Not back to Redwood Hills, not back to my mom, not back to us. We haven't heard from him since."

I reach over and take Ronan's hand, so big and strong, yet defenseless to the pain.

"I'm so sorry he did that. What did you guys do?"

"My mom tried to get in touch with him. Begged everyone that he knew to help us find him, but I didn't want to find him. Didn't want anything to do with him anymore. Eventually, I had to tell my mom to stop trying to contact him and let it go—let him go. But by that point, the bills were piled up, and our car was repossessed."

Ronan shakes his head at this, like he's trying to shake the memory.

"That's when Colin came in. He was my dad's best friend, the best man in their wedding. But their friendship was destroyed like everything else during my dad's drinking. By that time, everyone had heard about my dad. My mom had been covering for him, but it couldn't last forever. The whole town pitched in to pay the bills, get our car back, and help my mom with the kids. And that's when Colin offered me a job at the sanctuary. Over the past couple of years, he's been more of a father to me than my father ever was."

He nods toward the animal enclosures. "This sanctuary isn't just a job—it saved my life. I would come here, look into the sky, and feel like I was meant for so much more than this."

My heart breaks for Ronan. I didn't have the same experience, but we all have pain and suffering in our lives. I have often felt the same way when looking at the stars.

Are we made for more than this? A resounding "yes" beats in my heart. Even if I don't fully understand it, I know this is true.

"You are made for so much more," I tell him. "We all are. Sometimes it's the awful parts of our past that lead us to where we're supposed to be. I don't know how your dad could've left you like that, but there's got to be a reason for it—a reason that we may not understand now but will all make sense one day."

Ronan lifts our joined hands to his mouth and kisses mine.

"Ronan? Sadie?" Ranger Anderson's voice rings out as the outdoor lights flash on.

If I could stop time, I would have about thirty seconds ago.

"We'll be right there!" Ronan calls back.

The moment is over. The rain has abated, and the storm passes with a low rumble. Ronan hangs the blanket back on the hook. Just when I think the magic is drifting away with the storm clouds, Ronan gives me a smile, and I know it's just the beginning.

When we reach Ranger Anderson, he's not alone. There's someone next to him whispering in an oddly intimate way. They both have rain jackets zipped up and hoods on, hiding their expressions. He jumps slightly when he sees us approaching, a tinge of guilt on his face. That's when I catch a glimpse of the ginger hair falling out from the oversized hood next to him. Ms. Hannon's familiar blue eyes lock with mine and without her dark green glasses, she looks like a different woman.

THAT NIGHT I climb into bed and pull my quilt tight. There's a soft hooting of an owl in the forest. The soothing melody works its magic, and before I know it, my eyes drift shut.

The dark haze gives way to a distinct coldness in the dim light. A deep, heavy panting fills the air. I see her white paws first. They're slowly climbing a rocky hill with a persistent rhythm. As she crests the top, a carved-out den nestled in the cavity of an ancient cedar tree welcomes her. It's the perfect shelter for winter hibernation. Her paw scrapes at the mangled wood, and she grunts several times before landing back on all fours. She shuffles into the den, turning around three times before dropping down to the hard ground. The scent of cedar and moisture scatters in the mist. For the first time, I see the creature lying wrapped in the earth. Her breathing becomes deeper. With a grunt, she rolls to her side, revealing a rounded, bulging belly. Everything goes quiet, and a ray of light surrounds her. Not a single breath breaks the void. Angel is pregnant. She closes her eyes, settling into a deep sleep. The tranquility darkens as the shadow rises over her. A murky hand reaches for her, and I try to stop it, but I'm too far away. I can't get any closer. Angel startles, lifting her head, terror shining in her eyes.

"No! No! No!" I scream.

Footsteps sound on the wooden stairs. The door swings open, and mom flips the light on. "Sadie, are you okay?"

My heart races as I get my bearings.

"Yeah. I just had a nightmare."

Mom nods and relaxes her shoulders. "Do you want to talk about it?"

Yes. No.

"No, it was nothing." Telling her makes it more real.

Mom looks doubtful, but she turns around and walks back downstairs to her room. I lay awake for a long time. Angel is not only going to have another cub, but she's in terrible danger. Somehow, I know it wasn't just a dream.

I have to help her.

THE NEXT FEW weeks are busy at the sanctuary as we prepare for the big Thanksgiving Festival. It's a fundraising event that happens every year, and it appears to grow bigger with each passing year. Sandy and I are setting up a large haystack, filling it with toys. It will serve as the "Find the Toy in the Haystack" game later in the day.

Ronan and Colin have been repairing the horse wagon for hayrides. Both look like they're ready to take the axe and cut it into firewood instead. Gia is here too, helping to paint signs and make things look more festive. She really does have a way of creating a scene. The place looks amazing. Brushing hay off my jean skirt, I go over to join Gia. She painted the sign in shades of brown, green, and red to look like an autumn sunset. With her lettering stencils, she is working on the "r" in "HAYRIDE."

"It looks great," I tell her.

"Thanks. I think it needs more red though." She examines her work. "Will you and Ronan be taking a hayride together?" She flashes me a teasing smile and raises her dark eyebrows.

Ronan and I haven't had any time alone since the night of the storm. People around school have started to notice us though. Ronan has been sitting with us at lunch now, and the other students just save the seat next to me for him. He waits for me at the end of biology, and we walk to our classes together. Sometimes I'll bring a breakfast pastry for him before school, or he'll bring an extra coffee for me.

"I don't know," I confess. "I hope so."

"What's going on with you guys anyway?"

"I have no idea." I look at Ronan as he helps Ranger Anderson adjust a wagon wheel. "Do you think I should say something?"

"Most guys I know don't want to have that conversation. He likes you. I'm sure of that." She finishes painting the curve of the letter. "If it feels right, say something. But I think it's only a matter of time before you two are an official item. And that makes me so happy because I love you both, and you guys are so good together."

I find myself thinking just how thankful I am to have found Gia here and formed a friendship with her. Not having Anna around was really daunting in the beginning, but Gia has been so welcoming. I'm not sure if I would have been able to survive this move without her. I watch as the first people start trickling in for the festival, including Ms. Hannon who stops to talk with Ms. Maggie at the pie stand.

Mom mentioned that Ms. Hannon has picked up more hours at the lodge. How much time does she really need for the gardens? Every time I'm here it seems like she's never in the gardens. Sometimes I feel like she's watching me.

"Ms. Hannon's the best," Gia says, completely oblivious to my suspicions.

Everyone loves Ms. Hannon, and the truth is that I'm finding myself drawn to her too. Even so, I just can't shake the odd feeling that she's hiding something. But I try to push it all from my mind as Gia and I walk over to the pumpkin-painting table. We are scheduled to work for the first hour, but then we are free to walk around and enjoy the festival. The time flies by pouring paint, washing brushes, and cleaning up a couple of smashed pumpkins that unfortunately didn't stay on the table.

After our shift is over, Gia and I pick the biggest caramel apples and walk around the vendor tables. There's a wood carving table with a variety of wood animals of all sizes.

I examine an exquisitely-detailed turtle. "I wonder if this man is the one who made the rabbit statue that's in the garden."

"I bet he is," Gia agrees. "These carvings are incredible."

I pick up a small bear. It fits squarely in the palm of my hand, and I run my fingers over the ridges. It's beautiful. I'm graze my hand over the smoothness of the rounded stomach when I remember the dream. Images of Angel and her pregnant belly flash through my mind.

Suddenly I feel dizzy, and my ears ring. Bright dots flash before everything goes dark.

———

I AWAKE to see Gia and Ronan standing above me, looking both shocked and concerned. I push myself up but fall back as something hard stabs into my hand.

It's the wooden bear.

A tiny stream of blood flows over it as I loosen my grip, noticing the puncture on my palm. The result is a sickening image of a bloody bear. *Angel*. Acid burns my throat.

My head throbs as Ronan lifts me up and carries me away. I close my eyes and bury my head in his chest, a deep feeling of dread pressing down on me.

When I open my eyes, I'm on the couch in Mom's office.

"Sadie," Ronan says, brushing the hair off my face, "are you okay?"

He's sitting on the floor by the couch. Lines of worry are etched on his face.

No. But, how do I tell him?

"Yeah," I reply cautiously. "I must have been dehydrated or something."

He doesn't look convinced but doesn't ask more questions. He takes my hand, rubbing his thumb over my palm. "I'm glad you're okay."

I give a weak smile.

"Sadie!" Mom comes over to the couch and feels my head. Gia and Dr. Allen stand in the doorway.

"Yeah, I don't know what happened. Probably dehydrated."

Mom examines me and takes my pulse. "You don't seem dehydrated, but we'll get you some water."

"I'll get it!" Gia volunteers and hurries down the hallway.

When she returns with the water, I take a sip.

Mom brushes my hair off my forehead. "Thank you all so much for your help. Could I have just a few minutes alone with Sadie?"

"Of course. We'll be right outside," Gia replies. Ronan follows her reluctantly out the door.

"What's going on, Sadie?"

I don't know if it's the exhaustion, but I don't want to keep the dreams from her anymore, at least not the last one. "The other night, I dreamt about Angel."

Mom sits back in her chair.

"She was climbing to her den to begin hibernation, and I saw that she's pregnant."

I don't tell her about the shadow or the terror in Angel's eyes. "Have you heard anything about her?" I ask cautiously. "Do you know if she's pregnant? I mean, wouldn't we have known before we left Great Bear?"

Mom puts her index finger to her mouth. "It's possible that she wouldn't have been showing when we left Great Bear. Cooper was about a year and a half, so if she mated over the summer, the timing would be possible." Her methodical reasoning confirms what I already know to be true.

"The spirit bears are in trouble."

"Sadie, it was just a dream."

"It was more than that. It felt real. Like a warning or a call for help."

Mom bites her lower lip. "I think it's best to try to forget about it."

"But you know, it's not the first time I've had a dream like this."

Mom bites her lower lip. "The dream you had about your father may have just been a coincidence. It may not—"

"You know it was more than that. The night before Dad was killed, I saw Dad running with Angel and the cub. I heard the footsteps of the poacher. And I saw the blood..." My voice chokes. "It meant something then, and it means something now."

She shakes her head in denial. "You had no way of knowing that blood was your fathers."

"I could have stopped it."

"No!" She wipes her eyes. "It was an accident. A horrible accident."

"It wasn't an accident. He was killed. And I could have prevented it."

"Sadie, it's not your fault." She wraps her arms around me, and I want to lean into her embrace. I want to let her shelter me, but I know deep down in my soul that the dreams were meant for me. They're telling me something.

But am I brave enough to listen?

CHAPTER NINE

The next morning, Mom goes into town to pick up local honey from the farmer's market. I stay home and try work on my textiles project. I envision the tapestry and the depth of colors, but my hands aren't cooperating. I keep sewing and then resewing the same stitches. My mind goes back and forth to the dreams.

A knock on the front door interrupts my thoughts. I open the door, and Ronan's standing there with his hands in his khaki pockets. When I go out on the porch, Rocky jumps out of the truck bed and races up to greet me. I shower him with hugs and kisses until I notice Ronan fidgeting next to us.

"Ronan, are you okay?"

"I should have asked you this a long time ago." He runs his hand through his hair. "What I'm trying to say is, Sadie, would you like to go out with me?"

"Yes." The word is out before I can even think about it. "Of course I do."

His smile returns. "I know this is short notice, and I'm not sure if you're up for it after yesterday, but would you want to have dinner tonight? I'm thinking we could go to High Point Lookout. It's one of my favorite places in Redwood."

"That sounds perfect."

"Great. I'll pick you up at five," he says walking back down the steps toward his truck.

"Okay, I'll see you soon."

I watch him drive off and run back to the loft to call Anna. For the moment, the dreams are temporarily pushed aside.

———

THAT AFTERNOON I am waiting on the front porch when Ronan drives up. He walks over with a handful of wildflowers. Purples, yellows, whites, and greens combine in the perfect arrangement. The scent of nectar drifts through the air.

"They're beautiful."

"You're beautiful," he says, with a slight shake in his voice.

I glance down at my white peasant top and long, olive cotton skirt. I have my blue-jean jacket with me, and I've pulled my hair back into a ponytail, tied with a loose golden ribbon. A few ringlets frame the edges of my sure-to-be-pink face.

"Let me put those in water for you," Mom chimes, peaking out the front door.

Ronan immediately straightens, and I laugh at his sudden movement, so different than normal.

"Have fun you two." Mom winks as she takes the flowers inside.

Ronan holds the door as I climb into his truck. A brown wicker picnic basket sits next to the blue-and-white-checkered blanket.

"Don't worry, I got the food from the diner. It's safe to eat," Ronan jokes.

I let out a dramatic sigh. "I was worried there for a minute."

We both laugh but it feels different today. There's an intensity in the undertone. I don't know if it's the fact that we are going on an actual date or that my feelings have grown so much over the past few months that it's hard to keep up with the roller coaster of emotions that seem to come and go. But something is different today.

After a fifteen-minute drive, we pull into a dirt parking lot at the entrance of a trail. Ronan opens the door for me, and I step out into the vibrant sun. The temperature is in the high sixties, a warm day for the end of November. He grabs the basket, blanket, and a small canvas backpack with safety equipment, including rope, a first aid kit, and a horn similar to the one Dr. Allen had that day with the mountain lion.

"Just in case," Ronan tells me, catching the apprehension that's clearly showing on my face.

I have to admit it does make me feel better knowing that we have the bag.

Ronan points out a small set of wooden stairs leading to a partially covered trail, and I follow him along the path until we reach a small clearing. In front of us is an incredible view of the Northern Mountain range.

"Wow." I shake my head in amazement. "This is amazing."

"It sure is." He scans the panoramic view of the mountains.

"You must have felt this the first time you came here too." I take in the scene before us.

"I get the same feeling every time I come here. It always feels like the first."

I have a feeling that everything with Ronan will always feel like this view—new and exciting. We settle onto the blanket and open the picnic basket. There's cold fried chicken, potato salad, coleslaw, deviled eggs, and a container of homemade chocolate chip cookies. My stomach rumbles, reminding me that I haven't eaten since breakfast. Ronan and I divide the food onto two plates.

"How did you find this place?"

"Actually, it was my dad. He took me camping one time, when I was eight." He looks out over the horizon. "We carved swords out of broken branches and played knights. He showed me how to cook hotdogs over the fire and how to build the best s'mores."

"Lightly toasted on the outside and gooey on the inside."

"Exactly. We slept in our tent, under the stars, and it was one of the best nights of my life."

"I'm sure it was for him too."

Ronan shrugs. "Doubt it. But there were days between the drinking that felt like I had a real dad."

"Would you ever want to see him again?" I ask.

Ronan's hand balls into a fist. "Sometimes I want to jump into my truck and drive until I find him. Give him a piece of my mind."

"I can understand that."

"I'll never do it though."

I feel relief at his words. "Why not?"

"Because he has another family now." He looks down at the ground.

"You would never want to hurt his new family." I run my hand down his arm.

"I know what it's like, and I would never want to cause the kids the same pain I felt."

I wrap my arms around him, and we sit in comfortable silence for a few minutes. As the sun begins to set, I lean back on my elbows taking in the orange autumn horizon. It's like our own private world here. Just the two of us. Ronan takes out his camera and begins snapping photos of the sunset from different directions. I enjoy seeing him choose the angle for his shot. He's completely immersed in the moment, and I remember the first time I saw his photos. The grey wolf photo from the sanctuary lobby was the first time I really saw Ronan. It occurs to me that Ronan so perfectly captured the wolf's spirit because they are so similar. He reflects the wolf—a beautiful combination of strength and vulnerability.

He turns and takes a couple photos of me. Surprisingly, I'm not embarrassed or uncomfortable like I would have been at another time in my life. I want him to see me. And I want to see what he sees in me. He sets the timer, and we take a couple photos together.

When the last of the color drifts behind the mountain, we both lay on our backs staring up into the sky. The stars sparkle bright against the dimming sky.

"What do you think?" he asks me.

"It's incredible."

He smiles and looks up into the sky.

"Ursidae," I whisper.

He stills for a moment. I wonder if he's thinking back to the roll call from those early days in school before the teachers knew that I go by Sadie. There's recognition in his brown eyes, and they are encouraging me to continue.

"My parents met at university, not long before moving to Great Bear. Then they fell in love, under stars like this, surrounded by the bears they were studying. Soon after, they got married, right there on the base with the research team as their only family. Every year on my birthday, my parents would sit under the stars with me and tell me how they wished upon a star for me. But not just any star, the brightest star of the Ursa Major constellation. Looking up into the northern sky, they would trace the shape of the great bear and wish for a child. I was the answer to their wish."

"Ursidae," Ronan murmurs. "Bear."

My name sounds so different coming from his lips.

"Yeah. It seems that before I was even born, I was destined to be among the bears."

He points to the Dubhe star in the constellation.

"It's the star I would always wish on those nights at the sanctuary."

The same star.

Silence falls over us as we watch the star shining on us from above.

"Sadie, do you think we—"

Ronan's question is cut off by the sound of a phone ringing behind us—three high-pitched pings.

"Who's there?" Ronan calls.

Branches snap as someone hurries through the trees. The image of the shadowed man from outside my window that first night sends a chill down my spine.

Ronan jumps up. "Who's there?" he calls louder.

I look around Ronan, and a man's shadow lurks between the trees. "He's there." I point at the shadow.

Ronan points his flashlight at the man, but he turns and runs before we can get a look at him.

"Who is that?" I breath heavily.

"I don't know. It's safe here. Could be a lone hiker."

"Should we follow him?" I surprise myself with my own words.

"No! Of course not, Sadie. It's probably nothing, but we should get going."

"Good idea." Could he be the same man who I saw outside my window?

We pack up quickly and hurry down the trail until we reach the truck.

THE DRIVE HOME IS QUIET. When we reach my cabin, Ronan walks me up to the front door. I look up into his tender eyes and take a step closer, feeling his warmth. I hug him and tension drains from his shoulders, his arms relaxing around me.

"I'm going to report what we saw to Colin. He'll know if there's anything to worry about. I'm sure it was nothing though." He sounds like he's trying to convince himself as much as me.

"Okay, that sounds good."

I'm about to tell Ronan about the shadowed man outside my window that first night when Ronan leans down and kisses me, igniting every nerve in my body. My arms wrap around his neck, pulling him closer, with the promise of many more to come. When we break apart, I feel breathless.

"Goodnight, Sadie," Ronan whispers, sounding as breathless as I feel. He kisses the top of my head in that protective and comforting way of his. All thoughts of mysterious shadows fade away so that only Ronan fills my thoughts.

"Goodnight, Ronan."

I climb the stairs to the loft and fall into bed with the memory of Ronan's arms around me and my lips still tingling from my very first kiss.

TWO WEEKS LATER, I'm sitting in biology, and my mind keeps drifting to Ronan—a common occurrence these days. Things have been great between us. He's distracting me from thoughts of dreams and strangers in the woods. I turn slightly and glance at him. He is slouched back in his desk chair, arms crossed over his grey Redwood Academy Baseball sweatshirt. He smiles back, and I feel the blush in my cheeks. It's almost too good to be true.

Movement around me breaks my daydreams. Everyone is taking out their notebooks, so I reach into my backpack for mine. My hand lands on a piece of folded paper.

Did Ronan put a note in my bag? Just the thought is enough to feel those butterflies in my stomach. I put my notebook on the desk and unfold the note on my lap.

GO AWAY!
YOUR DAD DIDN'T STAND A CHANCE AROUND YOU.
MURDERERS AREN'T WANTED HERE.

The bold, block lettering screams at me. Someone knows about Dad's death. A loud humming sounds in my ears, and the room begins to spin. I grip the desk but feel myself swaying in my seat. A hand touches my arm, and I pull away. My throat burns, and I know I'm going to get sick.

I need to get out.

I crumple the note in my fist and jam it into my backpack before hurrying out of the classroom. I burst out the hallway door as Ms. Hannon's voice rings in my ears. Once outside, I get sick by the bushes.

A familiar hand touches my back, and I look up into Ronan's worried eyes.

"I have to get out of here."

"Okay," he says without hesitation. "Let's go."

He helps me into his truck and gives me his water bottle. He darts a quick look at the school building before stepping on the accelerator.

We drive fast in a direction that I've never been before. We're both silent as he maneuvers the back roads until we finally come to a stop at a trailhead. Silent tears flow down my cheeks.

Ronan gets out of the truck and walks around to my door. Opening it, he reaches for my hand, and I follow him to the trail. We push through overgrown weeds and bramble and climb up a large hill. When we finally reach the top, I recognize the spot immediately. In the clearing is the large rock from the photo of the grey wolf. This is where Ronan was the night he took the photo of the wolf. Without him saying anything, he leads me to the rock, and we sit down together. He wraps his arms around me, and I can feel how special this place is for him. It's like he's revealing a part of himself, and I'm finally ready to do the same.

I no longer feel afraid to tell him about what happened that awful day.

"I saw something today, in class, and it reminded me of my dad's death." I want to pull out the note but can't bring myself to open it back up yet. "It was all my fault."

Confusion replaces the concern in his eyes.

"What's your fault?"

"My dad's death."

Ronan gently brushes the hair off my face, leaving streaks from the wet strands. "It can't be your fault. You could never hurt anyone."

His utter confidence in me makes the guilt even more painful. I know it's time to tell him the whole story. I tell him about the first day I met the white bear I now call Angel. I tell him about our days together and everyone's surprise at our friendship. I explain how Angel was pregnant and would deliver her cubs that winter. I was so excited. But the excitement didn't last.

"When that Spring came, we realized that Angel had just one cub. And he looked so much like her—the same white fur and deep brown eyes. He was adorable." I smile remembering his too-large feet and lopsided gait.

"Sounds like he was a lot like me when I was younger," Ronan jokes.

"He was perfect. But I started having these dreams."

"What kind of dreams?"

"Sometimes it would be Cooper running through the forest with something chasing him, but I couldn't see what. I would get glimpses of blood, and it scared me. I just wanted them to go away, so I pushed them out of my mind." I take a deep breath knowing where the story is going.

Ronan rubs my hand with his thumb in a comforting way. "You don't have to tell me anymore if you don't want." There's so much compassion and understanding that my heart squeezes in my chest. And that's when I know I love him. Looking into his eyes, I know I need to tell him everything.

"The night before my dad died, I had another dream. There were flashes of movement through the woods. Black boots stomped through the forest. Angel fished with Cooper in the moonlit riverbank. She caught a fish and carried it over to him, and then stretched out on this large rock. Cooper was holding the fish up high, proud of the catch. They were so happy. Then everything changed. Angel went rigid looking into the woods. Her ears were alert. I saw movement in the trees and then a bright light and loud bang. Then blood was all over the ground."

I shift on the rock. "It was a call for help. I was so scared something would happen to the bears that I never imagined it would be my dad instead."

"The next day, we got an alert that there was a poacher in the forest. That day, which seems so long ago now, was the worst day in my life. I followed Dad and the research team into the forest. When he noticed I was with them, he tried to make me go back to the base with my mom and the others, but I wouldn't go. I begged him to go after Angel. I told him where they were—where I saw them in my dream. The rest of the team went in another direction, and I pleaded with him to go the other way. He didn't want to do it. He wanted to take me back, but he finally gave in. Just a few minutes later he was dead. He died trying to save Angel and her cub. The poacher shot him. The blood I saw in the dream was his."

Ronan pulls me closer and kisses the top of my head. "It's not your fault. There's no one to blame but the poacher."

"He wouldn't have been there if I hadn't made him." I close my eyes, and when I open them, Ronan is watching me, giving me the time I need to grieve.

"The research team said that the spirit bears were all safe, but they didn't catch the poacher. We still don't know who it was. I hate knowing that he's out there somewhere."

"I hope he's caught and pays for what he did."

I only nod, but my hope was lost a long time ago.

Ronan looks almost as pained as I feel, and I lean into him, setting my head into the crook of his neck. "We'll figure it out, okay? We'll do it together."

And for the first time in a long time, I feel an ember of hope beginning to burn.

CHAPTER TEN

Dread weighs heavy on my chest as I walk through the front door to the cabin. Mom is pacing in the living room and twirling her hair—a sure sign of stress. She mumbles to herself before noticing me at the door.

This isn't good. I have seen my mom like this only a couple of times, and there has never been a good outcome. I brace myself for whatever she's about to say.

"The school called and told me that you ran out of class today. That there was some incident, and you just left the building without telling anyone. Drove off with Ronan, and no one had any idea where you went." Her voice shakes.

How could I not have realized that the school would call her? I don't respond right away because I know she's not finished yet. She builds up everything she wants to say and then says it all at once and in one breath. I know it's easier to let her get it all out and then try to talk with her.

"I don't know what's going on with you. You're worrying me."

She surprises me by not saying anything else. She sits on the couch and crosses her legs. I try to pick my words carefully. How is it that it takes a call from the school to finally notice that something is wrong?

Instead of fighting back like I normally would, I join her on the couch and slouch into the soft cushions. "It's the dreams."

Her brows furrow in confusion. "I don't understand."

"The dream I told you about wasn't the first."

"Okay. But Sadie, people have dreams, and that's normal."

"They're not normal dreams. It feels like a message or something."

"What are the dreams about?" Mom turns to me.

"Angel is running, trying to escape, but I don't know what from. At first, I thought it was the bad memories coming back, but now I know it's more than that. She's in danger. I think all of the spirit bears are. But I don't know why. And it feels bigger than just the bears. Like it's about us too."

She takes a deep breath and opens her eyes. "Sadie, I need to tell you something." She speaks slowly like she's trying to find the best words to continue. "I know now that I shouldn't have kept this from you. I thought I was doing what was best for you. You suffered so much with Dad's passing, and I didn't want you to have to deal with anything else right now. We're making a fresh start here, and I wanted you to be free." She shakes her head as if trying to erase it all.

What has she been keeping from me? I feel my anger beginning to rise. I do everything I can to control it though because I need to know what she's talking about.

"What?" I ask as calmly as I can. "What *didn't* you tell me?"

"It's the bears, Sadie. They're disappearing. I've been in touch with Papa Jay and the research team. They said it was just one or two missing at first, but they're disappearing faster now."

"What? Are they dying?"

"No. No bodies have been found. They're just disappearing. But no one knows where they're going or what's happening to them."

"But they're hibernating now," I protest. It doesn't make sense.

"They're disappearing from their dens. And it's only happening to the spirit bears. The other black bears don't seem to be disturbed. The team thinks it's an illegal poaching operation, but there's no evidence, so they can't do anything about it."

My heart thumps in my chest. "The same poacher who killed Dad?"

Sadness swims in her eyes. "We don't know."

"But Anna didn't say anything."

"I asked her not to."

My hands are now shaking with anger. I force myself to look her straight in the eyes. "You purposely had everyone hide this from me? You don't have the right to do that."

"I'm sorry, Sadie. I thought I was doing what's best for you—"

I stand up, unable to remain seated any longer. "What's best for me? How would you know what's best for me? You don't even know me anymore. I've been dealing with these dreams, and you've known about the spirit bears all along."

Mom twirls a strand of her hair until it knots around her finger. "Sadie, I'm sorry. It was wrong to keep this from you."

I walk to the window. I want to stay mad—I am mad. But I also understand why she did it. Don't I try to do the same thing? Don't I try to protect her from additional pain too? With the dreams clear in my mind, I hear the call again—the call for help.

"I want to go back."

Silence.

I turn back to her, my courage rising. "I want to go back to Great Bear."

At her stricken look, I continue. "Not move back. Just go back for a few days. Over Christmas break."

She blinks back tears and nods her head. "Okay. That could be good for you."

"Okay? That's it?" I expected an argument. While one part of me wants nothing more than to be back in Great Bear, there's another part that can't imagine being there again with the haunting memories.

Mom gets up and starts to pace again.

"I'll talk to Mama Rose and Papa Jay and arrange everything. I'll book your flight for the day after Christmas if this is what you really want?"

The question hangs in the air until I finally stand.

"Book the flight for two," I tell her walking out of the room. "Ronan is coming with me."

I WAKE the next morning to the ring of my phone.

"Good morning," Ronan says, voice heavy with sleep.

"Morning."

"Are you doing okay?"

Well, that's a loaded question and not something to talk about over the phone. "Can I get a ride with you to school?"

"Of course. I'll be there in a half hour."

"Okay, see you soon."

I pull on my brown corduroy skirt, cream-colored cable knit tights and hiking boots. I pair the skirt with a cream-and-pink knit sweater and add my bear-paw necklace and gold crescent-moon earrings. I stop in the kitchen for a bagel and then wait on the front porch. When Ronan pulls up in his black truck, he opens the passenger door for me. I hop in and strap on my seat belt.

As soon as Ronan climbs back into the driver's seat, I fill him in on everything that happened the night before.

"So when do we leave?" He asks me.

"You really want to come with me?"

"I'd go anywhere with you, Sadie."

The weight on my chest lifts ever so slightly. "Then we leave the day after Christmas."

"Okay, let's do it." He glances at me. "And don't worry, my mom will let me go."

I stop holding my breath. "So did you get in trouble yesterday?"

"Nah, my mom just asked if everything was okay. I told her it was, and she dropped it. I know she has so much going on with the kids that I'm the last one she worries about."

Something in the way he says this makes me sad. He talks about the kids like he's their guardian, which he is a lot of the time.

When we arrive at school, we're both called to the principal's office during first period. Our principal, Mrs. Buonaparte, is a large woman with a rounded, ruddy face and southern accent from her days growing up in Texas. Tom, a grey tabby cat, follows her through the hallways and is known for not only keeping mice out of the school, but for leaving them as presents by her office door when he finds one. Gia tells the story of how Mrs. Buonaparte took him in from the streets of

Texas, and now they are inseparable. She's an imposing figure, but underneath her stern expression is a kindness that I have noticed when she's interacting with the students. I don't know what to expect as we enter her office, but I'm hoping her kindness wins out.

She's behind her desk writing in a notebook when we knock on the open door. Tom is curled up on her generous lap, gently purring.

"Please come in," she says without looking up. "Take a seat."

We sit in the two wooden chairs across from her desk. There's a spring poking out of the red seat cushion, and I adjust to minimize the pinch.

"Would you like any water?" She waves a hand toward the water cooler by the side wall.

"No, thanks," Ronan answers, and I merely shake my head.

"Alright, then go ahead and explain what happened yesterday." She runs her fingers along Tom's back in a soothing way and looks at us expectantly.

Ronan clears his throat, but I speak first. "I got sick, and Ronan helped me. I'm sorry. We shouldn't have left like that."

"You are right about that. I'd like to remind you that we have a wonderful nurse right here at the school. Why did you feel the need to leave the building?"

"That was me," Ronan says. "I offered to take Sadie home since she wasn't feeling well. But we would never do it again."

Mrs. Buonaparte narrows her eyes, but then smiles. "I appreciate your honesty. I'm not going to suspend you this time, but you both will serve three detentions after school. And I'd like to remind you that at no time are students allowed to leave campus during the school day."

"Yes, Mrs. Buonaparte," we say in unison.

"You may return to class." As we leave, Mrs. Buonaparte watches me closely before returning to her notebook.

Ronan and I walk silently through the hallway until he stops and pulls me over just outside the biology classroom. "Sadie, I need to tell you something."

"Okay." The seriousness in his tone puts me on edge.

"Listen, I know you're scheduled for the sanctuary this evening, and I wanted to tell you before you found out from someone else. I was going to tell you yesterday, but with everything going on... Colin has decided to put Cosmo up for adoption."

"No. He can't." The truth is that he can and often routinely puts horses up for adoption so they can rescue and foster new horses.

"Why Cosmo?"

"He says that Cosmo is still young and would make a good horse for a family or riding program." Ronan leans against the wall.

"But why can't he do that at the sanctuary?"

Ronan looks pained as he shrugs. "I'm sorry, Sadie."

"Why does it feel like my whole world is falling apart, piece by piece?"

Ronan takes my hand and turns to go into the classroom, but I stop him this time.

"Ronan, I have something to tell you too. About yesterday."

This causes a wave of worry to cross his face.

I pull the note from yesterday from my bag and hand it to him. I hadn't planned on doing it this way, but I can't keep it from him any longer. "I should have showed you yesterday but couldn't bring myself to read it again."

Ronan's jaw clenches as he reads the note. "Who gave this to you?"

"I don't know." I take the note back and return it to the small, zippered compartment of my bag. "Yesterday in class I reached into my bag to take out my notebook, and it was there."

He crosses his arms over his chest. "Sadie, this is serious. We should go to the police."

"No."

His mouth hangs open. "Why not?"

"I had to talk with the police so many times after my dad's death that I just can't. I don't understand the note. Maybe it's a joke."

"It doesn't sound like a joke."

"But who would want me to go away?"

His looks around the hallway like it holds the answer. "I don't know."

Callie comes to mind, but she couldn't possibly do something like this. Even if she does want me gone, how could she possibly know about Dad and the poacher? Then, I remember that Mom not only told Ronan about Dad's death but also Ranger Anderson that day in the exam room.

"You don't think Ranger Anderson would have said something to someone?"

"Never." Ronan leaves no doubt in his immediate answer.

Ranger Anderson has been nothing but kind and supportive since we've arrived. But the image of Ranger Anderson whispering intimately with Ms. Hannon the night of the storm flashes in my mind just as the classroom door swings opens and Ms. Hannon steps into the hallway.

"Are you two planning on coming to class today, or do you have somewhere more important to be?"

I follow Ronan, but Ms. Hannon stops me outside the doorway, turning her back to block the classroom. "Sadie, is everything okay? I was worried about you yesterday."

"Yeah, I'm fine." I shift from one foot to the other.

"Okay, well I hope you know that we all care about you here at Redwood Academy. If you ever need anything, or want to talk, you only need to ask." She gives me an encouraging smile.

I nod and hurry into the classroom.

THE QUESTIONS CONTINUE AT LUNCH.

"Everyone was talking about it." Gia pops a potato chip into her mouth.

"I mean if you guys want to cut, you gotta do it right," Evan jokes. "One day, I'll show you how it's done."

"Sadie wasn't feeling well and needed to leave," Ronan explains.

"Yeah," I agree. "I got sick outside and couldn't go back in."

Nether Gia nor Evan looks very convinced, but thankfully they drop it. Being the last day of school before Christmas break, the cafeteria sounds even louder than normal. There's a group of boys tossing M&M candies in the air and competing to see who can catch the most in their mouths. With only two classes left before the break begins,

I'm not sure how much the teachers are going to be able to accomplish.

"You're at the sanctuary today, right?" Gia asks as she pops a chip into her mouth.

"Yeah, from six to nine. Ronan's giving me a ride after detention."

"Oh, great. Could you guys give me a lift too? I'm supposed to help Uncle Eric with some paperwork." Gia rolls her eyes. "It's my mom. She's just making sure that I'm staying busy, so I don't 'ruin my life again' as she so lovingly puts it."

Since that first night at the diner, Gia has filled me in on a lot of what happened in Maryland. Her family lives in an affluent community outside of Baltimore. She began hanging out with a troublesome crowd, and she was caught shoplifting makeup. Gia was let off easy since her dad is very influential in their community, but unfortunately it didn't end there. Gia was at a party a couple of nights later, and it was busted by the police. In addition to the alcohol, they found large amounts of drugs. Gia swears she did not know about the drugs but was still charged with drug possession. She vehemently denied it, but after serving three months in juvenile detention, her parents decided to send her to live with her older sister Meg and her family in Redwood Hills.

Meg married a California businessman the year before. They met while he was working in the same office building during a two-year stint in Baltimore. Meg was interning in the financial department of the large corporation and ran into him during a lunch break. From what Gia says, the rest was history. They now have two little girls and what Gia describes as "the perfect life." So Gia came to Redwood Hills to live with them, her parents hoping that Meg will rub off on her. The fact that Dr. Allen, Gia's mom's brother, also lives here is another benefit. While Gia was angry about the move at first, she loves living here now.

I can't blame her. Redwood Hills has found a place in my heart, too.

I PLAN what I'm going to say to Ranger Anderson while we drive to the sanctuary later that afternoon. The thought of Cosmo leaving feels like I'm losing yet another friend, and I wonder how much more I will have to lose. After Ronan drops us off, Gia decides the paperwork can wait, and she walks with me toward the sanctuary. Along the way, we bump into Ranger Anderson, but my plans are derailed when I see another man with him.

"Girls, this is Nathan Lewis, the new handyman." Ranger Anderson gives us a weak smile. "He moved here a few months ago from San Francisco."

Nathan has a medium build and greasy, black hair. Patchy stubble dots his pale cheeks and chin. His brown baseball hat conceals most of his face and shadows his eyes.

"Nice to meet you," Gia says, shaking his hand.

"Hi." I hold out my hand, and he grins at me, a gold tooth glinting from his mouth. He has a tight grip, and my fingers are crushed against a large ring on his right hand. I pull my hand away quickly.

Nathan's phone rings from his belt clip. I recognize it as the same sound from the woods during the picnic with Ronan.

"We need to go." I pull Gia toward the sanctuary with me. "I don't want to be late with the treatments."

I have no doubt that was the same ring from the night of our first date, but is it just a coincidence?

"That's odd," Gia says when we're far enough away that they can't hear us. "I've never seen him before. Redwood Hills is a small town, and Ranger Anderson said Nathan moved here from San Francisco a few months ago. Wouldn't we have seen him around? I know I would have remembered him. He's kind of creepy, isn't he?"

Yes, he is.

CHAPTER ELEVEN

I awake to that feeling that is only there on Christmas morning. There's a sacred silence hanging in the air and a feeling that today is different than any other day of the year. Nothing can change that. It's like for just this day, all things are possible. Everything and everyone can have a new beginning and a chance to experience something so special that we wait all year for it to come.

Airline tickets rest on my bedside table. Ronan and I will be leaving first thing in the morning. A heavy knot tightens a little more around my chest as the day nears—a dread of the unknown.

As I get dressed, I spend more time getting ready than normal. I slip on my emerald green sweater dress, allowing the soft material to hug my body. I pull on black crop leggings with soft fleece. I leave my hiking boots by the closet today and step into black flats instead. I lace their satin ribbons up my ankles.

Sitting at my vanity, I apply thin black eyeliner and a sparkly mauve eyeshadow with care. I swipe my lashes with black mascara, and my green eyes brighten in vivid contrast to the darkness. A peach glow highlights my cheeks and lips.

My mom and I have a quiet morning at the cabin. We exchange presents and watch *Miracle on 34th Street*, a tradition of ours, before heading over to the research center for Ms. Maggie's Christmas party.

When we arrive at the center, little white lights twinkle in the windows. A large evergreen wreath hangs on the front door. Its red-and-green plaid bow gently blows in the cool breeze. I reach for the door, but Ms. Maggie swings it open with a lavish bow.

"Merry Christmas, my beautiful girls!" She embraces us in a massive hug. She's wearing a bright red velvet dress with a white faux-fur wrap over her shoulders. Her hair is teased and curled so that it almost looks like it's a whimsical silvery nest above boldly-shaded eyes and ruby lips. Christmas tree earrings hang form her ears, swinging at each movement. She looks a bit like an eccentric Mrs. Claus. A glass of eggnog is swirling dangerously in her hand, and she smells of sugar cookies as she leads us over to join the rest of the party.

Ms. Hannon is sitting by the fireplace, a group of children around her, listening intently as she reads from an old-fashioned Christmas Treasury. The red in her hair glimmers in the firelight, making her look like an enchanting fairy. She catches my eye, but I quickly turn away, heading toward the kitchen area. I don't see Ronan, so I fill a plate with roasted turkey, scalloped potatoes, green beans, and hot crescent rolls. I eye the assortment of pies and decide that I can fit a small slice of the apple pie on my plate. I slide onto a chair in the corner and watch everyone.

The research team, sanctuary workers, and park employees are all here with their families. Kids are running around while their parents chase after them. One little boy is sneaking chocolate mints off the table and then hiding underneath to enjoy his treat. On the other side of the room, Mom is talking to Dr. Allen in a familiar way that turns my stomach. Her short blond hair is full of bouncy curls next to her black dress.

I spot Ranger Anderson leaning against the doorway staring at Mom in much the same way that I was. Watching him leaves no doubt about how he feels, but I can't tell if Mom has any similar feelings.

I walk to the front window and look out into the dark night. Christmas lights illuminate the trees, creating a magical atmosphere. It doesn't matter how long I have been here now: the redwood trees always remind me that I'm in the presence of something extraordinary. The Redwoods are the tallest trees on Earth. Some of the trees are more than 370-feet high, about five stories higher than the Statue of Liberty and anywhere from 800 to 1,500 years old. With the lights, it's like an enchanted fairyland.

Strong arms wrap around me, and I close my eyes, letting his warmth comfort me.

"Merry Christmas," Ronan whispers in my ear.

I turn in his arms, kissing him. "Merry Christmas."

His mouth hangs slightly open. "Wow. You're so beautiful."

"You look pretty good yourself."

Ronan is dressed in dark blue jeans and an olive-green sweater with three buttons at the neck. His hair is brushed and still a little damp like he just got out of the shower. His pine scent drifts into the air.

He smiles at me. "Come with me."

I shoot him a questioning look.

"I want to give you your Christmas gift."

As we walk toward the stable, a light shines from inside. Ronan pulls the sliding barn door open, revealing hundreds of white Christmas lights draped from the ceiling. Each strand twinkles and reflects off the metal latches like a constellation.

"It's incredible." I can't stop staring at the lights.

"I knew you'd love it. I did promise Colin that I'll take them down and turn off the heater before leaving tonight, but it's worth it."

The blue-and-white picnic blanket from the run-in shed is in the center of the aisle in front of Cosmo's stall. Two wrapped presents are sitting on the edge of the blanket, with a card sitting on top with my name on it. I add Ronan's gift to the blanket and walk over to Cosmo's stall, wondering when it will be my last time to see him. The horse is wearing a Santa hat connected to his halter, and he has an annoyed look.

"Yeah, he didn't appreciate the hat." Ronan points at Cosmo. "Just a little longer boy, and we'll take it off, okay?"

Cosmo nuzzles my shoulder, and I rest my head in the curve of his neck. I'm going to miss him so much, but I don't want to think about that today. I give Cosmo one quick kiss on his nose and join Ronan on the blanket.

"Merry Christmas, Sadie," Ronan says as he hands me the larger box first.

I unwrap the reindeer paper to find a distressed wooden photo frame. Turning the frame around, reveals a photo of me watching the sunset on our first date. I realize that I've never seen the pictures from that day. It's taken from the back and angled to catch my profile. I'm leaning back on my elbows as I look toward the mountains, the sunset just reaching the peaks in the distance. The colors are a mixture of orange, red, and gold, highlighting my features. I look content. My hair is illuminated by the light, causing my golden curls to look like a part of the sunset. I have never seen myself in this way before.

After Dad's death and the guilt that followed, I built a wall around my heart. But Ronan has been breaking down that wall since we met. He sees me as I am, and he loves me. He doesn't have to say it. I can see it in this picture. I see it in the way he captured me in that moment. At some point I lost that love for myself. Seeing myself through Ronan's eyes, I finally begin to recognize myself once more.

I lean over and hug Ronan. "Thank you."

His smile is like a salve for my bruised heart. "You still have one more," he reminds me, handing me the small box wrapped in the same reindeer paper.

I feel something slide inside as I unwrap the package. It's a white jewelry box with a horse logo on it. Lifting the lid, I find a star-shaped golden charm with "Cosmo" etched on it.

"It's beautiful." I check under the tissue paper looking for a chain for the charm."

"It's a charm for Cosmo's halter."

"Oh. It's perfect for him." I walk to Cosmo and snap the charm on his halter. "Whoever adopts him will be so lucky."

Ronan stands next to me at the stall door. "I talked to Colin, and he's letting me work off Cosmo's adoption fee. He said that he can stay here, as long as I work to help with his board and care. Colin has the papers and everything ready. He's yours, Sadie, if you want him. I mean, who else could bond so well with a horse named Cosmo? Ursidae and Cosmo. You two were meant for each other."

I turn to him. "Are you serious?"

He laughs. "Yup."

I throw my arms around his neck. "Thank you. Cosmo and I aren't the only ones meant for each other."

We share another warm kiss, and his fingers tangle in my hair.

Cosmo nudges between us with his nose.

"Alright, we can take this off now, boy." Ronan removes the Santa hat, and Cosmo gives a playful shake of his head.

"Ronan, these gifts are everything. Thank you."

"Seeing you happy is all the thanks I need."

Cosmo snorts, and I give him a peppermint treat before returning to the blanket.

"Okay, your turn." I hand Ronan his present, a shirt-box sized box wrapped in brown paper with a red bow tied around the center.

Ronan lifts the lid and pulls out the 16 x 16-inch tapestry.

"This was my textiles project this semester. It's for the bare wall in your office."

He examines the blend of greens, browns, golds, reds, and blues that recreate the wolf photo hanging in the sanctuary lobby.

"It doesn't seem right that your artwork is everywhere except in your office."

"It's incredible, Sadie." He runs a finger over the knotted fabric.

I let the moment settle into my heart. We've given each other something that shows how we see the other—gifts that reflect who we are. There's so much happiness in knowing that you are seen and loved as you are. It's a true gift to respect and cherish that in someone else.

The lights flicker twice.

Ronan sighs. "I better turn those off."

"I wish we didn't have to, but we should get back to the party too." I fold the blanket and place it on the welding table as Ronan unplugs the lights and checks the outlets. He takes my hand as we begin to walk back to the lodge.

As we pass the garden, a shadow moves by the floodlight to our left. I drop Ronan's hand and strain to see the figure in the darkness.

"What's wrong?"

I don't answer him and run toward the shadow, pulse thumping with the rush of adrenaline. The shadow moves slowly around the main lodge, out of sight. I pick up my pace and hear Ronan's footsteps behind me. As I turn the corner of the lodge, I hit something hard and fall to the ground, a sharp pain searing my knee.

"Ow!" I hug my knee to my chest as the shadow looms over me.

"Get away from her!" Ronan yells, smashing into him, knocking him to the ground. He crashes into the flower garden, hitting his head on a large grey stone.

The lodge door flies open, and a high-pitched scream echoes into the night. I roll over to see the man face down on the ground. On the steps, Ms. Maggie bursts into tears, and Ms. Hannon puts an arm around her, whispering in a soothing tone. Mom and Ranger Anderson are kneeling on the ground, checking the man's vital signs. There's blood puddling around his head of dark hair.

"Slowly turn him over." Mom's voice is controlled.

My chest tightens as I take in the unconscious form of Nathan Lewis.

THE NEXT MORNING my alarm sounds at 4:30. I barely slept more than fifteen minutes at a time during the night. Mom was able to stop the bleeding, and Nathan was taken by ambulance to the emergency room. There are no fractures, but he has a head wound and a concussion. Ms. Maggie is staying with him for now. I didn't realize how close they are, but I guess she is like a mother to everyone around here. But the question remains: What was Nathan doing in the woods last night? And is he the same man from the first night and the picnic? This sends a shiver down my spine.

"Sadie, it's time to go. You don't want to miss your flight," Mom says, opening the loft door. "I have some eggs and toast ready for you."

Did she sleep at all last night?

"I'm getting up."

Mom carries my suitcase to the stairs. "Are you sure you still want to go? It was a rough night. We could postpone until tomorrow or another day."

I shake my head. "I want to go today."

"Okay, don't be too long getting ready. We don't want to be late for your flight."

"Mom?"

"Yes, hun?"

"Everyone assumes it was an accident last night—that we ran into Nathan, and he fell. But why was he in the woods?"

She rests the suitcase on the floor. "Ms. Maggie said he likes to take a walk in the evening."

"But it was dark. Where was he walking to in the dark?"

"People have their own preferences. Apparently, Nathan enjoys the woods at night."

"Isn't that weird?"

She shrugs. "I don't know. I guess it's a little odd for him to be in the woods that late, but I'm sure he has his reasons."

Why does it feel like his reasons can't be trusted? I consider this as I climb down the ladder of my loft bed.

Mom picks up the suitcase. "I'll see you downstairs."

I don't ask her anymore questions, but a big one still remains: What was Nathan's reason for being in the woods?

I try to put it all out of my mind because today I'm going back to Great Bear.

<hr>

WHEN OUR SEAPLANE lands in Great Bear, the smell of fish greets us.

"We're here," Ronan says, his voice still groggy from sleeping during the flight.

"Yeah." I look out across the water at the trees in the distance. "I thought it would feel weird, but it doesn't." I've been dreading coming back, afraid that everything from Redwood would somehow disappear.

"Does it feel like home?"

"I don't know."

A breeze hits us, and I tighten the green, wool scarf around my neck. It's thirty-one degrees, about twenty degrees colder than it is in Redwood Hills. The cool air prickles my cheeks, making me feel so alive. Ronan pulls his black wool beanie over his ears. His nose is already a light shade of pink. A wave of gratitude washes over me for his presence.

Walking down the dock, we see Papa Jay and Anna coming toward us. Anna looks the same in her dark denim jeans and white puffer coat. Her black hair is in a braid, hanging over her shoulder, with a red wool cap on her head. Anna's face lights up when she sees me, and before I know it, I've dropped my bag, and I'm running toward her. We wrap each other in an affectionate hug, and everything feels right again.

"I've missed you so much." Anna says, squeezing me tight.

"You, too."

"Wait." She pulls back, wiping a stray tear. "I need to meet Ronan."

I laugh. "Of course." My two worlds are about to collide.

Papa Jay joins us, wrapping me in a warm hug, and I allow myself to rest my head on his chest. His presence has always been one of protection and support. Whenever I needed anything, I knew I could always rely on him to be there for me. I look up and see him looking at Ronan, who is standing a bit back, looking unsure of what to do.

"Papa Jay, Anna, this is Ronan." I take Ronan's hand and pull him into our circle.

"It's a pleasure to meet you." Papa Jay extends a hand.

"You too, sir." Ronan shakes his hand.

"No need for sir. Papa Jay is just fine." He smiles that comforting smile of his.

"And I'm Anna." She gives Ronan a big hug.

I probably should have warned him that the Whitefield family likes to hug. Ronan is smiling though, so he doesn't seem to mind.

An hour later we greet the rest of the Whitefield family and the research team. It is a bit surreal seeing everyone again and introducing them to Ronan. I've never had a boyfriend, and it's strange to introduce people who I've known my whole life to the person who has quickly become one of the most important in my life.

"Are you okay?" I ask Ronan.

"Yeah, just a little nervous. It's like I'm meeting your family for the first time, and I want them to, you know, like me." He runs a hand through his windblown hair.

He's adorable. "They're going to love you. I think Jasmine might already be a little in love with you." I tease him about Anna's thirteen-year-old sister ogling him. "They'll love you like—"

I was going to say, "like me." But we haven't said that yet. I mean, Ronan did write "Love" on his Christmas card, and our actions show it all of the time, but the actual words haven't been spoken.

"Ronan, want to play some ball?" Anna's older brother Jason calls to him from across the room, holding up an old worn-out baseball. Jason is just over six-feet tall and muscular. His black hair is cut short in a military style, and his black sweats and hoodie make him look like he's in a military training exercise.

Ronan jumps up in his excitement. "Yeah! That would be awesome. Let me grab my glove."

"Wait—you brought your glove?"

"Of course." He looks at me like that was the craziest question that I could have possibly asked him. I mean, who doesn't bring a baseball glove in the middle of winter on a trip to the Great Bear Rainforest?

***

WHILE RONAN and Jason play catch outside, I settle in the kitchen with Mama Rose and Anna, waiting for Papa Jay to join us. Mama Rose is in a bright red-and-white smocked dress reaching to her ankles, with black hiking boots poking out from underneath. Her black hair is tied back in two braids, each falling on her shoulders. Her round face is makeup-free, but her cheeks have a rosy glow that never seems to disappear. Her brown eyes are bright with laugh lines surrounding them. Wooden flower earrings hang from her earlobes. The red of the petals blends with the green stem and leaves.

Mama Rose clears her throat. While it's nice catching up with everyone, there's a reason I'm here, and we all know it.

"How's your mom?" Mama Rose sits on the round, wooden kitchen stool.

I drink the last swig of my green tea. "Okay. She really likes the research center and the clinic."

She takes a sip of her tea with a knowing nod.

"Mama Rose, have you ever heard Mom talk about a man named Dr. Allen?"

Her mouth forms a tight line, but she says nothing.

After a few seconds, I continue. "He's the scientist, the lead researcher in Redwood Hills. Apparently Mom went to school with him at Berkeley. I've never heard her say anything about him until the move, but they seem close."

"I know who he is." She nods with a hint of sadness in her eyes. "He's a man of much ambition, but I'm afraid to say, not much heart. When he was here last year—"

"He was here last year?" I interrupt, looking between her and Anna. Anna shrugs her shoulders, but Mama Rose lowers her head slightly.

"He was here for something concerning the spirit bear research. I'm not sure what, but he and your mom spent almost the whole day in the woods. I didn't have the chance to speak with him long, and he was gone before I could say goodbye." She folds her white cloth napkin into a small square.

"Where was I?"

"It was the day you and Anna went fishing with Papa Jay and Jason."

I look at Anna, but she looks as confused as I am. "Mom never said anything. Why wouldn't she have told me? If not here, then why not when we moved to Redwood Hills. It doesn't make sense to hide it."

"I don't think she was hiding it, Sadie. It's just we all were going through so much with your father's passing, and she wasn't really herself."

"That's not an excuse." I twirl a strand of my hair. "There's something I don't like about him."

"Sadie, I do understand how you feel, but just be careful not to judge him too quickly."

"I don't trust him."

"You twirl your hair just like your mom." She points to my hand. "Maybe talking with her about Dr. Allen would help."

I drop the strand of hair. "Maybe."

Papa Jay comes in, and I get the feeling that he overheard our conversation. He takes a seat on the stool next to Mama Rose. "Sadie, we are happy you decided to visit. It is good to have you back here. Hopefully we can unravel this mystery with your help."

My chest tightens as I remember the call for help I felt from the dreams. I look down to the floor. "Last time I tried to help, Dad died."

"Sadie," Mama Rose says, "you are not to blame. The only one to blame is the poacher. Remember that."

"That's easier said than done."

I tell them about my recent dreams. While they know about some of my past dreams, they don't know about the dream I had before Dad's death.

"We suspect poachers, but there is very little evidence." Papa Jay's voice is serious with a hint of fear.

"The same poacher?" I find myself wanting the answer to be yes. If it is him, we have another chance to catch the man that broke my family.

Papa Jay closes his eyes for a moment. "We're not sure."

"We're hoping," Mama Rose says gently, "that by being back here you may remember something from that day that could be a clue. But we don't want to put you in a situation that brings you more pain from the memories so please tell us if—"

"I want to be here."

A mix of relief and dread washes over her face.

I'm supposed to be here. I can feel it.

I just hope that whatever we discover will lead us to the answer we need to save the spirit bears and finally put the questions surrounding Dad's death to rest.

CHAPTER TWELVE

The log burns in the firepit outside the research base. The musky scent hangs in the air. The crackling of the wood and the smoldering barbeque creates a serene peace on the stone patio. Ronan seems to be adjusting to the cooler temperature. He laughs with Jason by the fire.

"Salmon?" I ask Papa Jay. He's standing over the grill with beads of sweat on his forehead.

"Of course. It is your favorite." His smile reminds me how much of a second father-figure he has been to me over the years.

I inhale deeply. "I've missed this."

"The fish or Great Bear?"

I sprinkle a little more seasoning on one of the fillets. "Both."

"Well, you know that we are always here for you—as will the fish." He winks at me.

"Papa Jay, there's something I want to tell you—about my dreams."

"You can tell me anything."

"I know. And I know you all understand how I have these dreams, but there's one you don't know about."

He puts the tongs to the side, giving me his full attention.

"The night before Dad died, I had this dream. Angel and the cub were running from someone. They were in trouble. And right before I woke up, there was blood all over the forest floor. I thought it was from Angel or the cub. That's why I made Dad continue to chase the poacher that day. I wanted him to save them. But he was the one that died."

"Sadie, there are moments in life that force us to fight."

"Fight the poacher?"

"Fight our own demons. You are not to blame for your dad's death. But you need to choose to believe that and fight the urge to blame yourself. You, my dear, are strong and have the biggest heart. You love with your whole heart—don't let guilt take that away from you."

"I want to believe you, but if I do, it's like I'm pushing aside the part I played in everything."

"Your dad would have fought to protect Angel and any of the spirit bears whether you asked him to or not. Your dad was a fighter. He fought for what he loved. While it was a tragedy, he is a hero."

I let Papa Jay's words sink in. "He is a hero," I say quietly.

"He always had a hero's heart." Papa Jay points to the center of my chest. "You share that with him."

"Me? I am nothing like a hero."

He gives a little chuckle. "One day you will realize how strong you are. Let your heart lead you, and you won't go wrong."

Anna joins us. "Papa, Mama said to bring the salmon to the table when it's ready."

"It's ready now." He slides the grilled fish onto the orange serving tray.

We join the rest of the family at the wooden table. Each of the chairs is a different color, as if representing the unique personalities of each family member. I sit on the teal-blue chair, and Ronan slides in the red one next to me. Anna sits in the purple chair on my other side. The room is full of windows and is airy but has a temperature-controlled mechanism that always keeps the room at seventy-two degrees. Sometimes it's nice having a bunch of scientists around because you know you will always be surrounded by innovation.

"This meal is amazing," Ronan says, finishing off his second piece of salmon.

Mama Rose smiles. "So glad you've enjoyed it. Papa has a way with that grill."

"You have a way with the green bean salad and sautéed rice," I remind her.

"That she does," Papa Jay agrees. "Ronan, tell us about Redwood Hills. Have you always lived there?"

"Born and raised."

"What's your favorite part of the town?" Mama Rose asks.

"The animal sanctuary for sure. I'm the assistant ranger there, and there's nowhere I'd rather be, but Great Bear is quickly becoming a favorite too."

My smile grows at his words. I suppose you can have two places that feel like home.

"Do you think your baseball team will do well this year?" Anna asks.

I laugh as the topic of conversation always seems to go back to their favorite sport.

Ronan has no trouble discussing the ins and outs of the upcoming season, and I let myself sit back and take it all in. I look through the windows and into the woods. The Sitka spruce and Douglas firs don't look like the Redwoods trees, but they provide the same protective canopy.

Under the trees and next to the patio are three tents for the campout. Ronan and Jason will have their own tents, and Anna and I will be sharing, just like we used to. I know they have all the cold weather gear set up for us. Winter was always my favorite time to camp out. Anna and I would curl up in the high-tech sleeping bags that the research team made for us and tell stories, sometimes fantasy, sometimes real. I wonder what it will be tonight. Probably a little of both.

After dinner Ronan, Anna, Jason, and I go down to the firepit. A few years ago, the team carved eight benches to sit around the fire. I've spent so many nights out here, under the stars. The four of us talk about Jason's university program. It has me wondering again what I would like to do after graduation. Since being at Redwood Academy, there is always so much talk about college and the SAT test and what's going to happen after graduation.

Will I stay in Redwood Hills? Or maybe come back to Great Bear? Or perhaps I will go somewhere completely new and walk my own path?

Ronan nudges me with his knee, interrupting my thoughts. "What do you want to do after high school?"

How can I put the muddled mess of my thoughts into words? "I don't know. The counselors at Redwood Academy are always talking about looking at colleges that have a major or area of study that you feel drawn to. So many people seem to know what they want to do. Gia wants to go into graphic design or advertising. You're always talking about applying to a pre-vet program, which I think is great. I can totally see you as a vet, but I don't know what I see for myself."

"Something with art or design?" he asks.

"Maybe. I don't know what I'd do with it."

"You still have plenty of time to figure out what you want to do," Jason reminds me.

"That's true," Anna agrees. "We still have another whole year before we need to decide."

She's right, even though I know she has been looking at college brochures for years. It feels like I'm falling behind everyone else.

"Ronan, do you know what schools you're applying to for a pre-vet program?" Jason asks.

He glances at me. "Not yet."

Will we stay together? What if we're on two completely different sides of the country or even the world?

I honestly don't know where I belong right now. There's a part of me that will always want to be here, in Great Bear, but there's another part of me that feels like Redwood Hills is my home now. There is even the smallest part that desires to go somewhere completely new. It's hard to know where you want to go when you're still trying to figure out who you are.

My thoughts wander as they continue talking about college, and it's not until Anna and Jason both go into the tents that I begin to clear my mind and come back to the present moment.

It's comfortable sitting by the fire with Ronan, but as night comes, I worry about whether there will be another dream. I'm torn between wanting one and being scared to have one.

Ronan slides an arm around me, and we watch as the embers sparkle in the pit. There's so much I want to ask him and so much I want to tell him, but I don't know where to begin.

"Thanks for bringing me here." His warm breath tickles my ear. "This place just feels like you."

Did Ronan just answer my question for me? I wish it could be that easy, but I know it's not. I know the decision for where I end up has to be mine.

"I'm glad you're here. You fit right in. I mean you and Jason are practically best friends now and have probably planned a baseball tournament for the Spring."

"A tournament is a good idea."

I give him a playful push, and he wraps both arms around me to keep his balance. Only he doesn't let go.

"Wow."

At first, I think he's talking about us but then notice that he's looking up into the sky. The aurora borealis shimmers in the distance. The red, green, and purple lights dance in the starry sky.

"Man, this is the holy grail of stargazing. You know where it comes from, right?"

Of course I know. I grew up seeing the northern lights with a group of scientists, but he sounds so excited that I can't help but want to hear it from him. I love listening to Ronan's passion for science, which is one of the things I find so adorable about him. Even though I grew up around scientists, I've never had a special love for it. It's interesting, but it doesn't grip me like it does Ronan or my parents.

"See, at any given moment, the sun ejects these charged particles from its corona, creating a solar wind. The wind slams into Earth's upper atmosphere like a baseball off a bat. It can be as fast as forty-five million miles per hour. You would think this would be catastrophic, but Earth's magnetic field protects us from the impact, redirecting particles in the atmosphere toward the poles. Every type of atom or molecule absorbs and radiates its own unique set of colors, like how every human has a unique set of fingerprints. Red is the nitrogen molecules. The green, oxygen molecules. And the pinkish purple is hydrogen and helium. I've also heard once that when the nitrogen atoms begin to decay, they can also emit a purple light. Either way, it's incredible."

He's still looking into the sky, and I rest my head on his shoulder.

"I bet you wish you had your camera." I imagine the incredible photos he would take.

"Not really." He shrugs. "I know I'll never forget this. With or without a camera, this image will always be in my mind."

I know the feeling. Being wrapped in Ronan's arms, in Great Bear, watching the aurora borealis. I will never forget this moment either.

"I love you, Sadie," he whispers, resting his head against mine.

My heart swells as I look up at him, his brown eyes soft and hopeful. "I love you too."

We kiss, and in that moment, I know that no matter what happens in the future, this is where I'm supposed to be right now.

"Look!" I point to the sky. Ursa Major shines bright right above us. "It's our star."

I FEEL THE COLD, wet ground soaking through my socks. The moonlight gives a delicate glow, illuminating her paw prints in front of me. I don't know where I'm going, but I know I need to keep following the path. There's a misty ice hanging in the air that clings to my eyelashes, making it hard to blink. A cloud of steam is coming steadily from my mouth. The prints are leading me somewhere, but I don't know where. Angel is standing not even ten feet in front of me, a ray of light overhead. I stop and look into her dark eyes. I take one step at a time, pausing a moment between each. I lean down and stroke her soft head, and she presses it against my chest. My heart echoes in the stillness, each thump providing new breath, new life. She lowers herself down and lays her head on the ground. Then I see it—a glint in the moonlight. I kneel, resting on my legs and pick up the object—a ring. Its silver is tarnished, weathered by the elements.

There's a symbol on the top, but I can't make it out. She lays her head on my lap, and I curl over, resting on her back. The cold is biting into my bones. I feel myself drifting away with the sound of Ronan calling my name in the distance.

I awake to the gentle sunlight drifting through the window and Anna's patchwork quilt wrapped around me.

My eyes dart around until I realize that I'm in her bedroom. The last thing I remember is lying down next to Anna in our tent. It was right after Ronan told me he loved me. I still can't believe we finally said the words. I replay the memory again in my mind, feeling Ronan close to me. The most perfect moment.

Then I remember the dream. Angel. The ring. It felt so real holding it in the palm of my hand. I pat my side where my coat pocket would have been and feel Anna's flannel pajamas instead. I roll out of bed and spot my clothes hanging on Anna's desk chair. Reaching into the coat pocket, my fingers curl around the heavy metal, and I sigh in relief.

Unclenching my fist, I take a good look at the ring. It needs to be cleaned to remove the tarnish. I've seen Mom clean silver many times with baking soda and warm water. If I can clean it, then I should be able to make out the symbol on top. I know this is the clue that we need. I carefully replace the ring in my coat, zipping the little inside pocket and walk out of the bedroom.

Papa Jay, Mama Rose, Jason, Anna, and Ronan are all in the living room. Each of them seems deep in thought. Ronan is sitting on the floor, back against the couch with his forehead scrunched with concentration.

"Hey."

Ronan jumps up and runs to me. "You okay?" He wraps me in a tight hug.

"Yeah, but you are suffocating me."

He releases me, and by the look of him, I really should be asking him if he's okay.

Everyone's looking at me, questions burning in their eyes. Mama Rose pours me a cup of tea, and I sit on the couch next to Anna. I move over to give Ronan some space to sit too, but he's pacing with nervous energy.

"What happened?" I ask.

Jason pulls his chair closer to the couch. "Anna woke up around two this morning and saw that you weren't in your sleeping bag. She came to check with us and of course, you weren't there either. Then we saw your footprints in the frost. We followed them as fast as we could. Luckily you weren't too far into the woods when we found you."

Anna holds my hand. "You were curled up in a ball covered in frost. Your lips were blue. You were out of it. We were so scared."

"I was in the woods? I thought it was a dream."

Mama Rose puts the teapot on the stove. "We think you were sleepwalking."

"Sleepwalking? But I've never done that before." The thought scares me—anything could have happened.

Concern is etched on her face. "Ronan carried you back to the base. Anna and I changed your clothes and put you into bed."

"Do you remember your dream?" Papa Jay asks.

Mama Rose hands me a teacup. I take a sip of the hot tea, and its herbal flavor invigorates me.

"I saw Angel and started following her. It's like I knew I had to follow her." I pause here, remembering the feel of the metal in my hand.

"What was she leading you to?" Jason asks.

"A ring."

He raises an eyebrow.

"What did it look like?" Anna wraps herself tighter in the yellow throw blanket.

"I'll go get it."

As I walk into Anna's bedroom, I hear their surprised murmurs. I return to the couch and open my hand, revealing the battered ring on my palm.

"What is it?" Anna turns it around in her hand.

"I don't know. I must have picked it up in the woods last night. It looks like there's a symbol on the top, but it's too tarnished to make out."

Mama Rose quickly mixes up the baking soda and warm water as Papa Jay examines the ring, turning it around between his fingers repeatedly. Instead of looking at the ring, my gaze lands on Ronan as he stares out of the window and into the woods. He hasn't said a word.

"Is he okay?" I whisper to Anna and Jason.

They exchange a look, and Jason leans closer. "He was really upset when you were missing. We all were, but it's hitting him hard."

I join Ronan by the window. "Are you okay?"

He finally looks me in the eye. "It all got real this morning."

"Ronan, this has never happened before."

"I know, but it's not just the dreams or the sleepwalking. It feels like we're getting into something that is really dangerous."

He's right. I can feel the threat hanging in the air. But instead of feeling scared, I feel more alive than I have in a long time.

"It's ready," Papa Jay calls from the kitchen.

We join them at the table, the now shiny silver ring sitting in the center. On the top of the ring is an ancient symbol of some kind. I look up at Papa Jay for answers, but his brow is furrowed.

"Does it mean anything to you?" he asks me intently.

"No." I shake my head, wishing it did. "I've never seen it before."

Anna begins searching online. "It's an ancient symbol for spirit," she tells us.

We are all deep in thought when I know what I need to do. I no longer feel the need to be in Great Bear, but rather I feel drawn to Redwood Hills. It's the last thing I would have expected. "I need to go home."

It's not lost on me that I said home.

At their questioning expressions, I continue, "I don't know how to explain it, but I have this feeling that the answer is in Redwood Hills."

<hr>

PAPA JAY GETS everything in order within the next couple of hours. I spend that time packing and saying goodbyes. It's so hard to leave everyone, especially the Whitefield family, but I know this is the right decision. Ronan has hardly said two words by the time we are settled on the seaplane for the first part of our journey home. There are dark circles under his eyes and an edge to his jaw that won't relax. Whatever he's thinking, he's not sharing it with me.

We arrive back in Redwood Hills around eleven in the morning, about eighteen hours after leaving Great Bear. Mom is waiting for us, and she runs to me as soon as she sees us.

"I'm so glad you're home safe." Her hug is tight, but I don't try to pull away.

"Let's get you two home," she says, smiling at Ronan.

He gives a weak smile in return and carries our bags to the Jeep.

The drive home is quiet. As we pull up to Ronan's cabin, he turns to me. "I can stay with you."

"No," I tell him, a little too quickly, "you need to get some rest."

He starts to object, but I put my hand up. "I want to go to Gia's New Year's Eve party at Dr. Allen's tonight."

Ronan looks shocked by this. The New Year's party is the last thing that must be on his mind.

"Sadie, wouldn't you rather stay home and get some sleep. We can catch up on everything and put on a movie," Mom says, a hopeful note in her tone.

"No. I want to go to the party." I turn back to Ronan. "We can meet around eight and head over together, if you're up for it?"

"Okay." He reluctantly gets out of the Jeep. "See you tonight." He leans back in and gives me a quick kiss before closing the door and walking into his cabin.

We drive the short distance to our cabin, and Mom parks the Jeep. "Mama Rose filled me in on everything, Sadie. I'm glad you decided to come home, and I want you to know that I'm here for you. Maybe Ronan's right, and you should stay home tonight."

"Ronan kept close to me the whole trip home. I could barely go to the restroom without him acting like the secret service, waiting just outside. I know things that night were scary. I'm scared too, but I need a break. I just want to do something fun." Now an idea begins to form. While the idea of Gia's party is a good distraction, it will also give me a chance to look for any clues I might be able to find at Dr. Allen's house.

"He's just trying to protect you, Sadie."

Part of me can see the sweetness in Ronan's actions, but I don't want a bodyguard. I need to figure out what's going on.

"I know," I say with a nod. But I also know that I need to do the next part on my own.

LATER IN THE EVENING, I study my reflection in the mirror. My eyes are pink from lack of sleep, and my skin is dried out and rough. My hair falls limp at the sides, and I pull it back into a ponytail. I have been going through all the motions and doing everything I know I have to do, without realizing that this is taking its toll on me. Just as I'm about to get up from my vanity, I pull out the ring from my bag. Turning it over between my fingers, I know I need to find the answer tonight. If I can find a way to search Dr. Allen's office, maybe I can find the evidence needed to connect him. It will be risky, and I don't think Ronan will agree to the plan. This is something I need to do on my own.

WINDOWS.

That's all I see when we arrive at Dr. Allen's house. While all over town there are rustic, cozy cabins, Dr. Allen's two-story glass house is much different. It gives me the creeps, just like its owner.

Doesn't he want privacy? Even though we're in a secluded section of the woods, windows go both ways. If people can see in, then Dr. Allen can also see out. How far he can see from the second story?

"You ready?" Ronan asks, looking like it's the last thing he wants to do.

My heart gives a tug. "Yeah. We don't have to stay long."

"Okay. It would be nice to have a quiet night at home with you, but you do look pretty great right now."

I look down at my short, gold satin dress with long sheer sleeves and hiking boots. "Maybe I should have left the hiking boots home. They don't exactly go with the dress."

Ronan smiles the first genuine smile all day. "I like them." He leans down and kisses the top of my head.

"An hour at most. I promise."

"Well, then let's go. The clock is ticking."

When we get inside, Ronan hangs up our coats, and I smooth my dress. Gia dances in a shimmering turquoise dress in the center of a dance party in the living room—gorgeous and so carefree. I get a sudden burst of jealousy. Why does she get to be carefree, and I have to carry so many burdens?

I need to find answers tonight so this can all be over soon. Ronan is still holding our coats and talking with Evan, who seems to be in the middle of a story. His stories always last a few minutes when he's so animated.

I look around, but everyone is absorbed in conversation. I tactfully make my way up the stairs. The rock music becomes muffled, and my senses are heightened. The windows provide an openness that you would think is releasing, but it's confining. I feel like all eyes are on me even though I don't see anyone. There's an open door at the end of the hallway, revealing a large rectangular room—Dr. Allen's office.

I walk into the room and gently close the door behind. I only have a few minutes before I need to get back downstairs. The sleek, black desk lamp shines on piles of papers strewn across his mahogany desk. I begin rustling through the papers, scanning every sheet for any clue of his involvement with the spirit bears or any sign of that symbol. Nothing. I begin shuffling through the drawers with increased desperation.

"Sadie, what are you doing?"

Gia's voice stops me in my tracks.

I turn toward the door and see Gia and Ronan standing there. Ronan's mouth hangs agape, while Gia takes in the situation, eyes narrowing at me.

"Oh, I was just...looking for something."

"You were looking for something on my uncle's desk?" Gia raises her eyebrows.

It hits me that this may have been a horrible idea.

I give a pained laugh. "Remember when I told you that the spirit bears are disappearing?"

Gia purses her lips. "Yeah. But what does that have to do with you being in my uncle's office?"

"We found a clue while we were in Great Bear. It's an ancient symbol, and we think it's linked to the disappearance of the bears."

When Gia says nothing, I continue. "So I just thought that with the symbol maybe..."

When I say nothing more, Gia crosses her arms. "What? That obviously this monster who's stealing the spirit bears has to be my uncle?"

"Of course not, Gia." Although that's exactly what I was thinking. "It's just that there's something odd about him. And when we were in Great Bear, I learned that he was there, early last summer."

"What?" Ronan looks more confused than ever, and I realize I never told him about that. I get the feeling that Gia is not the only one upset with me right now.

Gia takes a few steps toward me. "I'm sorry, Sadie. I didn't realize that everyone on the planet has to tell you about their travel plans. I'm planning a trip to Seattle with my sister and her girls in the Spring. Is that okay with you? Please tell me if you approve." Her words drip with sarcasm.

"You know that's not what I mean."

Ronan runs a hand through his hair. "Sadie, I know you're trying to find answers, but you can't let your feelings for Dr. Allen send you on a wild-goose chase. Maybe it's time to let it all go."

His words are a knife in my heart.

"This was such a mistake," I murmur.

Relief crosses his face, misunderstanding the intention behind my words. "Why don't we just go home? We both need to get some sleep. We aren't thinking right."

"No. This was a mistake." I wave my hand between us.

I run out of the room before my resolve falters, and I bump into Dr. Allen in the hallway.

He catches me before I fall. "To the rescue again."

I pull away from him and run down the stairs.

I'm almost out the front door when Evan stops me. "Sadie, where are you going?" He takes one look at me and senses the gravity of the situation.

"Can you give me a ride home?"

"Of course."

As Evan pulls out of the drive, I turn back and watch Ronan standing at the open front door, looking like someone punched him in the gut. Tears burn my eyes, and I promise to make things right.

CHAPTER THIRTEEN

Over the next week, I avoid Ronan and Gia as much as possible until Ronan and I are scheduled to work the early shift Saturday morning. It's our first time together since New Year's Eve. I debate whether I could call in sick and stay home, but as much as I would like to, I know that would not be fair to the animals.

I arrive at the sanctuary, check in, and begin the horse treatments. I bring Cosmo in first, needing his presence and comfort. Mom started him on an allergy treatment plan due to mild asthma. He gets four crushed Zyrtec with his morning feeding, and it appears to be helping his breathing. I lead him into the stall and sit on the bench right outside his door.

I crush the tablets into his grain, well-aware of Cosmo's intent stare. He is still a little protective over his food, like so many of the neglected rescues, but he is getting better with trust—a lesson I could learn from him. I have been avoiding Ronan and Gia to protect myself. I want to say "yes," but the doubt creeps in.

"How did things go so terribly wrong?" Tears well up in my eyes, blurring the bucket in my lap. When tears begin to fall into the mix, I place the bucket in the feeder and watch Cosmo gobble it down. I sit back on the bench and cover my face with my hands. My sobs are enough to quiet Cosmo and shake the bench.

The bench creaks loudly, and the faint scent of pine is a knife to my aching heart. "Sadie, please talk to me."

"Ronan, go away."

He doesn't move. "Did you read any of my text messages?"

When I don't say anything, he continues. "I never meant to say that I don't believe you or anything. When we found you in Dr. Allen's office, going through his drawers, all I could think was that this needs to stop. I don't want you in the middle of whatever is going on. I don't want any possibility of you getting hurt. Seeing you the way you were in Great Bear...I've ever been so scared in my life."

I'm so glad he didn't go away. Hearing his voice and feeling him so close makes the loneliness of this past week seem like a distant memory. But I want him to be my partner in this, not my bodyguard, and I need him to understand this.

He takes my hand. "Ever since that night in Great Bear, something has changed."

I wrap my fingers around his. "Something did change. I can't just stand by while the spirit bears are disappearing. When they were in trouble that awful day with the poacher, I persuaded my dad to save them. And now he's not here anymore. I've regretted that day so many times. But now, I feel like this is my chance at redeeming his death. I may not be able to change the past, but it's my chance to stop what's happening now. I need to make sure the spirit bears are safe and that they have a future."

"But I want you to be safe."

"Ronan, we can't live our lives always worrying about being safe. Accidents and tragedies happen all time." I know this too well. "I want you to be with me in this. I need you to be."

Ronan shifts on the bench and exhales a deep breath. "Okay, but you have to trust me. You can't hold anything back anymore. I love you, and I will always worry about you and try to protect you."

I look into his deep brown eyes and smile. He's a protector. That's who he is. Asking him not to be a protector is asking him to be something other than who he is. If I want to be loved for who I am, then Ronan deserves the same.

"I will," I promise.

He leans in to kiss me, but Cosmo chooses that moment to swing his head over the stall door and nuzzle my shoulder.

"Alright, I'll leave you two alone." Ronan laughs. "I'm going to start the avian treatments."

I rub Cosmo's nose. "Okay. I'll see you in a bit."

I watch him walk through the stable door. My heart beats strongly for the first time all week.

<hr>

AFTER I FINISH the horse treatments and feeding, I stop by the avian enclosure, but Ronan isn't there. I find him in his office, sitting at this desk and staring at a spreadsheet on the computer.

I walk over to the desk and sit on the edge, inches from Ronan. "Is that the wolf data?"

He nods. "Yeah. The pack is stable but there's been more blanks in the tracking system recently."

"Is it something to be worried about, or does that happen with the tracking system?"

"I don't know. I mentioned it to Colin, but he didn't seem to think it means much. Maybe an issue with the tech."

While Ronan's love for animals is evident in all of his interactions at the sanctuary, his eyes brighten with even the mention of the wolves.

"Hopefully, that's all it is." I glance at the wall tapestry hanging on his wall. A perfect fit.

"Hopefully. I'm sure I'm worrying about nothing." He turns off the computer.

"Do you want some pizza? I saw some in the center earlier. I bet there's extra that we can warm up."

He gives me a sideways smile. "I have a better idea."

We pull into the parking lot of the diner, and I refuse to get out of the car.

"Come on, Sadie." Ronan holds my door open.

"Gia might be working."

He shifts his feet. "She is working. That's why we're here."

I'm probably the last person she wants to see. "I can't talk to her."

"That's exactly what you need to do." Ronan's voice is firm.

He's right, and I know it. But that doesn't make it any easier. "I've thought a lot about what happened on New Year's Eve, and Gia doesn't know everything that's going on, only bits and pieces. It must sound crazy to her. I need to tell her everything, so she understands."

"Well, I know everything, and it still sounds crazy," he quips.

I take his hand, and we walk into the diner. It's bustling with townspeople, and we wait a few minutes before being seated at a small table by the kitchen. Gia comes through the kitchen door carrying a carefully-balanced tray. She serves a family of four, making sure to spin the plates a little before sliding them in front of the two kids. As she turns back to the kitchen, she spots us. For a brief instant she freezes, but then she comes our way.

She gives a shaky smile before taking out her notepad.

"Can I get you something to drink?" she asks, avoiding eye contact.

Ronan clears his throat. "Sure, I'll take a root beer."

"And for you?"

"I'm sorry," I blurt out.

Gia stops writing. "Me too! This is all so stupid. It was such a weird night. I blame New Year's. Evan and I were dancing and well, that's a whole other story."

Evan? I remember how Evan seemed a little quiet and not himself when he drove me home. But with everything that happened, I didn't question him.

"Want to come over after you get off tonight? We could catch up."

"Yes!" Gia exclaims without hesitation, and my nerves relax knowing that our friendship is deeper than this fight.

When she returns to the kitchen, Ronan has a big lopsided smile on his face.

"What? Do you want me to say that you were right?"

"Without a doubt."

"Fine. You were right, I guess, but I was going to talk to Gia anyway."

He tosses a balled-up napkin at me, hitting me right on the nose. I laugh and begin to ball up my own. "Oh, you're on!"

For the first time in a long time, we don't mention the spirit bears, mysterious notes, or Dr. Allen. We enjoy the moment, feeling like kids again.

LATER THAT NIGHT, Gia and I are up in the loft, and we share the pie slices she brought from the diner. "Ms. Maggie should really have her own bakery," I say, savoring the warm cherry filling.

"Agreed." Gia takes a large bite. "I love what you did with the walls."

I look around my loft at the varying shades of green I painted the walls this week. It's a mixture of deep tones and cool vibes.

"Painting helped me to release some emotion this week."

"I see. That was quite the emotional turmoil."

The emotions are still somewhat raw, so I change the subject. "So, what's going on with Evan?"

Gia puts her plate on the side and settles on the fluffy white rug, looking up at the ceiling. "I have no idea. It's Evan, you know, and he can't handle any kind of real relationship."

"Relationship?" What am I missing here?

"We almost kissed," she explains. "We were dancing and joking about who we should kiss at midnight, and then he leaned down and was about to kiss me when Ronan interrupted asking if I knew where you went."

"Wow. Did you want him to kiss you?"

"I don't know. At the time I did, but now I'm kinda glad he didn't."

I never pictured Gia and Evan together before, but it does make sense. They would be an energetically fun couple.

"So, anyway," she continues, "by the time we found you in the office, I was already in a mood and may have taken it out on you." She sends me an apologetic look.

"It wasn't just you. I was in a mood too." I lay down next to her on the floor. "I need to tell you about something."

She rolls over to face me.

"I need to start at the beginning." We spend the rest of the night catching up on the events of the past year.

THE NEXT MORNING, Ronan and Evan come over, and the four of us research the ring in my loft. Ronan filled Evan in on everything, and it's nice to have everyone together and on the same page. Gia is spread out on my bed, scrolling the Internet for any information about the bears in the news while Evan is sitting on my desk chair eating the last remaining slice of Ms. Maggie's pie. I claimed the window seat, looking into the woods just as much as searching the Internet.

"The white fur of the Kermode bears, spirit bears, is the result of a double-recessive gene unique to this subspecies. A single nucleotide replacement in the melanocortin-1 (Mc-1r) receptor portion of the gene produces adenine instead of guanine, which results in the white fur, often held as the holy grail of genetics," Ronan reads from his spot on the floor below the window seat.

I close my laptop and turn to him. "I thought you were searching through the news from British Columbia?"

"I was but then remembered the genetics homework Ms. Hannon gave us. It's a case study on the spirit bear. Good timing, huh?"

"It's weird," Evan says between bites. "Almost too big of a coincidence."

"It is," I agree.

Ronan seems more skeptical. "I guess, but it makes sense in the genetics unit."

"I don't know." There are times when I catch Ms. Hannon staring at me, like she's gauging my reaction or something. "Could she have assigned the genetics assignment for a reason?"

Ronan puts the genetics packet back into his backpack. "Why would she do that?"

"I don't know."

Gia takes a sip of her soda. "She would know about your parents' research with the bears and how close you are to them."

Evan stretches his long legs and leans against the wall. "You did find the first note during her class."

Everyone is quiet until Ronan speaks. "I'm not sure Ms. Hannon is the answer to all this."

"I know," I say, trying to dismiss the thought. "I'm still thinking that the ring is the key to figuring it out."

Evan and Gia exchange glances, but neither say anything.

"The symbol does look familiar," Gia says. "I wish I could remember where I saw it."

I grab the bag of chocolates from the floor and pop one in my mouth. "It's like I know the person behind all of this is here. But how do we find out who he is?"

Evan holds up a finger. "Or she."

"What?"

"It could be a woman." Evan says this like it's obvious.

I was only thinking about male suspects before, and now I fear I might have missed the mark.

"But it's a man's ring," Gia says.

Ronan sits up straighter as he stares intently at the screen of his laptop. "There's a local listing for a San Francisco Fraternity of Valor. The symbol looks similar. I need to enlarge it."

We look at the image—an identical match to the symbol on the ring.

"Nathan is from San Francisco," Gia reminds us.

Could it be Nathan?

"The dude you hit on Christmas?" Evan asks Ronan.

Ronan cringes. "Yeah." Then he looks at me. "He is from San Francisco."

"He hasn't been back at the sanctuary since Christmas. I know he was released from the hospital, but I don't know where he went. Do you?"

"No. I could ask Colin."

"Maybe he would know something." I sit up straighter. "That first day Gia and I met him, when I shook his hand, I felt this object digging into my skin. It could've been a ring."

Evan considers this. "Yeah, but a lot of people around here are from San Francisco, and a lot of people wear rings, especially university rings."

Evan is right, but I don't want to let Nathan off so easily. "But maybe that's where you saw the symbol, Gia, and just didn't realize it at the time."

She shrugs. "Maybe."

"And he's just really, really creepy." I'm a firm believer in intuition.

"Colin doesn't like him much either," Ronan says.

"What else does it say?" I ask, swinging my legs over the window seat to see his screen.

"The mission of the Fraternity of Valor is to develop men of courage in the face of battle. To establish a strong and honorable community of like-minded men who strive for unparalleled achievement in scientific endeavors. To support each other in unified scientific research, discovery, and entrepreneurship."

We let this sink in for a moment.

Gia climbs down the ladder on my bed and sits next to Ronan. "Are there any photos?"

"Just a couple. But I don't recognize anyone in them."

Evan and I join them on the floor.

I point to the top of the screen. "Try the research tab." He clicks it, and several links pop up. The first references the Pacific sea otter as a keystone species. The next is an article about coastal erosion. The third—

I read the blurb: "Implications of the melanocortin-1 (Mc-1r) receptor of the Kermode bears shed new light in human genetic engineering."

I suck in a breath as Ronan clicks on the third link, which reads:

The San Francisco Fraternity of Valor is leading a scientific revolution in the field of genetic engineering. The recent acquisition of genetic material from the Kermode bear is allowing for the sequencing of its genome. This advance provides the springboard for unlimited scientific revelations in genetic engineering. The research is unprecedented and carries the opportunity to create a global change in the way scientists view genetics. Moral and ethical standards will be questioned.

I stand up and start pacing. "Genetic engineering is a path the team at Great Bear always tread cautiously. Papa Jay would always say, 'just because we can do something, doesn't mean we should.' This research could cross the line of what's considered ethical research."

"Maybe they're using the spirit bears for research." Ronan's words hit hard.

I pull the genetics packet out of Ronan's backpack. "Maybe Ms. Hannon did give us this assignment for a reason."

"What do we do?" Gia asks.

"Let's talk to her tomorrow."

Everyone agrees, and we spend the rest of the morning delving into the Fraternity of Valor.

AT SCHOOL THE NEXT DAY, we learn that Ms. Hannon has taken a leave of absence and will no longer be teaching biology, leaving all our questions unanswered. With no way to get in touch with Ms. Hannon, we need to find another way. But another way isn't as easy as we thought.

By the middle of March, we don't have any new leads or clues. Ronan and Evan are busier with baseball, leaving me and Gia researching on our own most days. Nathan officially resigned his position at the research center and said he is going to visit family in Oregon. He never returned to the center after Christmas, leaving me wondering what he is hiding.

Things have been unnervingly quiet. There haven't been any more threats. I haven't had any more dreams about the spirit bears, and the research team in Great Bear haven't found any new leads.

I have been putting in extra hours at the research center because of the Spring Fling fundraiser happening later today. It was a lot of work to prepare, and Ranger Anderson insisted that I take the day off and enjoy the festival. I have a feeling Ronan has something to do with that, and I'm curious what he has planned. It's a warm day, and the weather forecasters are predicting low seventies and sunshine—so a perfect day.

I put on my light pink short-sleeve dress with my faded white jean jacket. I leave my hair down today, loose curls falling halfway down my back. I fasten my gold feather earrings and clip the bear-paw necklace around my neck. I'm hoping today will be a day to relax and just enjoy.

I slip on my hiking boots, grab my bag, and head downstairs. My mom is in the kitchen wiping down the windows. She's in a cute floral dress with a white sweater. Her short blond curls are held back with her black sunglasses.

"I thought you had to work?"

She jumps slightly at my entrance. "Oh, I took the day off. Figured we could go to the Spring Fling together."

So she's the one who got me the day off. I'm a little disappointed as I was hoping it was Ronan's surprise, but I am happy that Mom thought about having a day together. I don't remember the last time we had a day together doing something fun.

"Oh, okay." I grab a few red grapes from a bowl on the counter. "Want to get going?"

She glances at the clock and the front door. "Let's wait a few minutes."

"For what?"

"Oh, I don't know," she says casually, walking to the fridge. She empties the beef stew leftovers that appear to have been in there way too long and throws another glance to the door.

"What's going on?" I ask as the sound of tires crunch on the driveway.

I walk to the front door. Mom follows closely behind, a huge, goofy smile on her face.

Colin gets out of his truck and walks to the passenger side and opens the door. I catch a glimpse of a black ponytail as a girl hops out of the truck.

"Anna!" I cry and run to her. "What are you doing here?"

Anna beams at me. "Your mom planned it. I can only stay for the weekend though, but wow, is this place gorgeous?" She stares at the cabin wide-eyed.

"Let me show you around." I grab her hand, and we hurry into the cabin.

After a quick tour, Anna changes into one of my dresses—a long, white one with puffy sleeves, blue flowers, and a wide leather belt around the waist. I help her curl her hair, and she adds a white Vancouver Canadians Baseball cap. Her loose curls fall over her shoulder in an effortless way.

When we arrive at the research center, the festival has begun. Townspeople mill about the vendor tables, stopping to browse the wood carvings, glass fusions, and craft items. Young children are laughing in the petting zoo, thrilled to feed the goats and play with the rabbits. Anna takes it all in as I show her around. When we pass the horse rides, she gets to meet Cosmo, who is patiently giving a young boy dressed as a cowboy a walk around the arena.

We walk by the food vendors and stop for homemade ice cream in waffle cones.

"Sadie!" Evan jogs over to join us, looking at our cones. "That ice cream looks amazing. I'll be right back."

"Who's that?" Anna asks.

"That's the one-and-only Evan."

"He's gorgeous." Anna stares at him while he chooses his flavors.

I roll my eyes. Whenever Anna meets a new guy, she thinks he's the cutest guy she has ever seen.

"What? I don't get to see many new guys in Great Bear. Let me have fun."

Anna and I giggle as Evan comes back with a gigantic, three-scoop chocolate ice cream cone.

"I bet you will never finish all of that," Anna says, her tone playful.

"Sadie, I don't think you've introduced me to your friend. She seems to not have much faith in my abilities," he says, winking at Anna.

A pink flush creeps up Anna's cheeks, but there is challenge in her eyes. This is going to be interesting.

"Evan, this is Anna, my best friend from Great Bear. Anna, this is Evan, perhaps the goofiest guy in Redwood Hills. But he is an amazing baseball player."

"I love baseball." Anna's face brightens. "What position do you play?"

Anna and Evan talk about baseball, and I admittedly zone out a bit looking around. I watch Gia over by the ring toss. She's playing with her nieces, looking like the most fun aunt in the world, which I'm sure she is. Her sister, Meg, watches over them all with motherly attention. I wave Gia over, and after a couple of words with her sister, she runs to us.

"Were you surprised?" she asks me.

"You knew?" I glance at Anna and Evan engrossed in conversation.

"Yeah, your mom told me the other day. So, this is Anna?" She nods their way.

"Yup. It looks like she is hitting it off with Evan. She's a huge base-ball fan, so it's basically love at first sight," I joke.

But Gia doesn't laugh. Could she be jealous of Anna and Evan? I know that Gia and Evan had that moment on New Year's Eve, but since then I haven't heard either of them say anything more. They act like they always have and seem to be clearly in the friend zone. Seeing Gia's face right now makes me wonder if there's something going on that I don't know about. I feel like it's time to introduce Gia and Anna before quick judgments are established.

"Anna," I interrupt the conversation. "This is Gia!" I pull her to my other side closer to Gia, putting myself between her and Evan. Disap-pointment crosses her face at the move, but she smiles at Gia.

"Hi Gia. It's so nice to finally meet you!"

"Same here," Gia says, a tense smile pulling her lips. She glances at Evan who's busy finishing the last of his cone, clueless to her pointed look.

"Awesome!" Evan points across the field and nudges Anna with his elbow. "The speed pitch is set up. Want to give it a try?"

Anna adjusts the rim of her baseball hat. "Absolutely."

Gia watches them as they walk away. "She's really cute."

Before I can ask her if there's anything going on with Evan, Ronan joins us, and I decide to keep it to myself for now.

"So were you surprised?" He kisses my cheek.

"Did everyone know but me?"

Ronan laughs, but Gia is still watching Anna and Evan at the speed pitch.

Anna throws what must be Jason's secret fastball and crushes the score. Evan looks genuinely impressed as he takes her baseball cap and turns it backward on her head. She adorably turns her head giving him a wink. He laughs, and they begin another round of throws. They really do seem to be having a great time together.

A couple of hours later, the sun is setting, and the five of us are eating at the Pit-Beef stand. Anna has naturally joined our group and is having the time of her life. But Gia is the quietest that I've ever seen her. I had no idea she had such strong feelings for Evan. Even though she hasn't said anything, it's written all over her face. Evan and Anna are outright flirting, and I know that Anna and I will be awake long after midnight rehashing everything. I feel torn with happiness for Anna and sadness at seeing Gia so miserable.

"I gotta go," Gia tells us putting her phone away. "The girls are having a meltdown, and they need their Auntie Gia."

She stands up to leave, but her turkey sandwich has barely been touched.

"You eating that sandwich?" Evan asks.

Gia sends him a cold look. "Nope." She throws it at him and stomps away.

He catches it with the kind of accuracy only the best ball players have and takes a big bite.

After the festival winds down, Anna, Ronan, and I walk into Mom's office. She's preparing blood vials and a syringe.

"I need to get some blood from the Pacific shrew. It shouldn't take more than a few minutes."

"Can I help?" Ronan asks, clearly thrilled at the thought.

"Me too?" Anna asks. She's always up for anything.

"Sure." Mom walks to the door, and Ronan and Anna follow. "Sadie, are you coming too?"

"Nah." I slide onto the comfortable couch against her wall. "I'll be right here."

I put the yellow-threaded pillow under my head and wrap the blue throw-blanket around myself. They laugh before walking out of the room and in the direction of an exam room. It only takes a few moments before I drift off to sleep.

Dusk settles in the forest. The giant trees are growing toward the clouds, creating an arching canopy overhead. There's a musty smell and the sound of heavy panting. Looking down, I see Angel snuggling a small cream-colored cub. The cub begins nursing, and her eyes are alert taking in her environment. A heavy, metal collar is strapped around her neck, exposing red, raw skin. Anger burns inside me, threatening to erupt. Another bear walks behind her toward a small rock formation when it suddenly jumps back, shaking its head. Shock collars. The sound of footsteps is coming from behind me, and Angel's ears turn toward the intruder. The other bear slaps the ground as Angel stands ready to charge as a glowing light illuminates the background.

"Sadie," Mom gently shakes my shoulder. "Time to go home."

My eyes blink open, and the brightness of the office temporarily blinds me. My heart is pounding. I have too much energy, a shakiness, and I can't stay still. Anna and Ronan are looking at me now with concern on their faces.

"What's wrong? Did you have another dream?" Mom asks, her voice breathy.

"She alive," I tell them in rapid breaths. "They all are. But they're not in Great Bear."

"Where are they?" Anna asks.

"Here."

The word leaves a hollow silence.

I knew I had to come back here, but I thought it was just to find another clue. I hadn't even considered the possibility of the spirit bears being here. Their shocked expressions tell me that they hadn't considered this possibility either.

Anna sits on the couch next to me. "Here?"

"Yes. In Redwood Hills. The trees in my dream were Redwood trees. These Redwood trees," I say, without hesitation or doubt.

A clatter sounds from the other side of the door. Ronan opens the door, and Dr. Allen is on his knees collecting surgical instruments from the hallway floor. His hands shake slightly as he puts each tool back onto the tray.

"I'm such a klutz." He shakes his head, avoiding eye contact with us.

"What were you doing?" Ronan's voice is more accusatory than questioning.

He gives a startled laugh. "I was restocking the exam rooms. We've been running low, and I wanted to make sure Dr. Foster has everything she needs."

"I'll help you finish restocking," Ronan volunteers, his protectiveness showing.

"Alright, girls, let's go home," Mom says, an edge of nervousness in her tone. She grabs her briefcase, and we follow her out the door.

WHEN WE CLIMB into the Jeep, we notice an envelope tucked into the door with my name on it. I recognize the handwriting right away, and I tuck it into my bag before Mom sees.

"I forgot the keys." She groans. "I'll be right back."

When she goes into the clinic, I pull out the envelope.

"Dr. Allen really has it bad for your mom," Anna says with a huff.

I show Anna the envelope, and her eyes grow wide. "Not another one."

I pull the note from its cover.

LEAVE NOW!
OR
YOU AND YOUR MOM
WON'T LIVE LONG ENOUGH
TO REGRET IT.

CHAPTER FOURTEEN

There is a whole new level of tension after the dream and the discovery of the last note. A strange quiet comes over our group, partially because Gia will barely speak to Evan and partially because of the idea that the spirit bears could be here in Redwood Hills. Mom used all the resources from the research center, but there isn't any evidence that they're here. Yet, I know they are. I can feel it.

It's the last week of April, and the whole school has been buzzing about prom. It's hard to focus on anything else knowing that the spirit bears could be here in Redwood Hills, but I can't ignore that prom has taken over the school.

Gia is going with Brad Knott, a friend and football player that she dated for a few weeks last year. But I don't think Brad is who she wants to go with. Evan has surprised everyone and decided to go solo. I wonder if that had more to do with Gia or Anna. Or neither. Maybe Evan is trying to figure out what he wants too.

Since I've never been to a prom, the whole experience is new. The girls are talking about satin dresses, up-do hairstyles, and smokey eyes. The end-of-the-summer bonfire has nothing on the madness surrounding the after-prom party Gia is hosting at Dr. Allen's house. To say I am dreading this part is an understatement. Just the thought of returning to Dr. Allen's house has my nerves rattling. Gia is on the prom committee, and the party has been in the works since the beginning of the year. It would be hard to change it now. Gia's sister, Meg, will be there too, and it makes me feel better to know it won't just be Dr. Allen.

The fact that I am sitting at my vanity finishing up my makeup seems a little surreal with everything going on with the spirit bears. The shimmery gold eye shadow and black mascara make my eyes look big and bright. I apply a few light swipes of peach blush to my cheek and matching lipstick. Running my fingers through my long, curly hair, I feel it flow freely down my back.

"You're so beautiful." Mom stands by the open door to the loft, her eyes shiny with unshed tears. I stand up and do a little spin, allowing the long, white satin to flow around me.

"It's perfect on you." She smooths the thin straps on my shoulders and kisses my cheek.

When I mentioned making a dress for prom, Mom suggested I wear her wedding dress instead. It's a simple A-line dress with a natural waist. I didn't know if it would feel right with Dad not being here, but wearing it now feels perfect.

"It's like Dad is here with us too."

She dabs at her eyes. "He will always be with us."

I know I can't go back and change what happened. I may not understand now why Dad had to die the way he did, but I know there has to be a reason. I'm learning we never get over losing someone we love, but we can continue to live.

"I love you, Mom."

A tear slides down her cheek, but she doesn't bother to wipe it away. "Love you, too."

A knock sounds at the front door, and Mom squeezes me tight before going down the stairs. She ushers Ronan into the living room, and I hear their muffled voices. I apply a touch of lavender essential oil to my wrists and neck before descending the stairs.

Ronan stands in his khaki pants and white button-down shirt with a navy sport coat. He has an olive-green tie, and his hair is combed to the side in a formal yet tousled way. This time last year I would never have guessed that I would be going to prom with a boyfriend who I love so much.

Ronan looks up at me. His eyes are soft and his smile big. "You're so beautiful."

I smile back at him. "Thank you."

Our eyes meet, and I want nothing other than time alone with Ronan tonight.

He slips the corsage of white rose and baby's breath on my wrist, and I pin his flowers to his coat. The white roses stand out against the navy blue.

"What, no hiking boots today?" Ronan asks, looking at my white high-heeled sandals.

"No." I laugh. "I figure if we're actually going to be dancing this time, you probably don't want me stepping on your toes with my boots."

"Good call."

"Oh, you two look so good together." Mom grabs her camera. "Stand by the fireplace. I want to get a few photos before you leave."

We pose while Mom takes more than just a few photos. When we are finally walking out the door, she stops me.

"Could you take this letter with you to the party? It's for Dr. Allen. Ms. Maggie asked me to give it to him, but he was already gone when I left the clinic."

"Sure." I take the small envelope and slip it into my overnight bag.

As we leave, I have a feeling that tonight is going to be a night to remember.

THE GYM HAS BEEN TRANSFORMED into an enchanting fairyland. Flowering vines cascade from the ceiling, reflecting the gold-and-silver twinkling lights strung around the walls. A local band is set up by the dance floor, and smooth melodies drift around the room.

Gia waves at us, looking as beautiful as I knew she would in her bright-blue mermaid-style gown with sequins. Her dangling silver earrings sparkle as she bobs to the music. Her dark hair is pulled up into a twist on the top of her head, making her look elegant and fun at the same time. As we make our way to the table, we pass Evan as he's juggling three oranges with a group cheering him on. He doesn't appear to be the least bit upset about being dateless.

Our round table is covered with a silky-white tablecloth with green-and-pastel flowers stretching out from the ceramic centerpiece. The white dinnerware is rimmed in gold, and the napkins are various pastel colors. A large crystal bowl with garden salad sits on the table, and there are servers bringing the main course to the tables.

I choose the white fish and rice entrée, and Ronan goes for the steak and mashed potatoes. Both look amazing, and we end up splitting and sharing them. It was a good choice as I don't think I could pick a winner between them. The cheesecake with raspberry sauce for dessert is just as amazing. After we finish eating, I look at the dance floor.

"I kind of wish the bleachers were still down," Ronan says, a twinkle in his eye.

I smile back at the memory. So much has happened since homecoming, but that initial spark and connection between us has only grown stronger. I lean over and kiss Ronan.

We were meant to be together. I knew it that first night gazing at the stars. Ronan puts his head against mine, and we sway as the last of the melody drifts around us. For a first dance, I could not have hoped for more.

WE GET to Dr. Allen's house a little before eleven, and there are already people milling around. Rock music blares through the open front door, and I catch a glimpse of Evan swinging his tie around like he's in a rodeo, hooting with laughter. He has always been the life of the party, but tonight he seems to be on a whole new level. I intend not to worry for once and to enjoy the party and time with Ronan and my friends. Gia and her sister meet us at the door, and we follow them through the crowded hallway.

"Oh, I almost forgot. Is your uncle around? My mom gave me a letter for him."

"Uncle Eric actually went to the research center, saying something about important work to do." Gia makes finger quotes when she says the words "important work." "But he shouldn't be home too late. I can take it for him."

I reach into my bag and slice my finger on the sharp edge of the envelope.

"Ow! Ah, paper cut." I hold my finger away from my dress and wonder how something so small can hurt so much.

Gia and Ronan both wince. They must understand.

Blood stains the corner of the envelope while Meg walks off to get a Band-Aid. I'm using my forefinger to apply pressure when my chest tightens.

The ancient symbol stares back at me with its piercing points and blackened curves. It's the same paper and handwriting of the threats. Ronan takes the envelope from me. His face reddens with anger, and his jaw clenches so tight it looks like it's about to snap. He tears the envelope open and reads the note.

"What does it say?"

He looks around and hands it to me, slipping the envelope in his pocket.

TONIGHT'S THE NIGHT.
ALL FOR THE GLORY AND POWER.

Gia is frozen next to me, white as a ghost. For a moment I'm afraid she's going to faint.

"You were right," Gia says. "My uncle—"

I wish more than anything that we weren't right. And then it hits me.

"My mom," I say looking desperately at Ronan. "She's there."

Gia's sister comes toward us with a Band-Aid, and Ronan grabs my hand, the pain no longer registering. "Let's go."

As we hurry out of the door, Gia watches us with heartbreaking misery on her face.

RONAN DRIVES AS FAST as he can to the research center. As soon as the truck stops, we jump out and run to the entrance to the clinic. It's dark, and a flash of hope surges through me with the thought that maybe my mom is already home. But then I see our Jeep parked on the side of the building.

Her office is empty, so we run down the hallway toward the exam rooms. A light is on in the second room, and I turn the handle, but it won't budge.

I pound on the door. "Mom!"

Silence.

Ronan grabs the fire extinguisher from the wall and slams it on the handle, snapping it off. He twists the inner lever and swings the door open.

A mountain beaver scurries across the floor and out the door, but I barely see it. My eyes are glued to my mom's body, lying on the floor, blood dripping from her head.

CHAPTER FIFTEEN

I hear Ronan calling 911 as rumbling thunder fills my ears. I check for a pulse and exhale sharply when I feel the rhythmic thumping in my mom's wrist. It's slow, but she's alive. I find gauze on the counter and press it to the cut on my mom's head. It absorbs the blood quickly, and I add more.

"An ambulance and the police are on their way." Ronan takes the bloody gauze and applies a fresh piece. We both hold pressure to the wound.

"Please God," I pray, "don't take her from me. Heal her."

I have the sudden overwhelming sense of regret and guilt that I didn't listen to Ronan earlier to contact the police. Could I have prevented this from happening? My throat burns as the familiar thoughts run through my mind.

"Sadie, don't do this. This is his fault and no one else's. We're going to catch him, and he's going to pay for this. For everything." Ronan gives me assurance, as if reading my mind.

Before I can answer, a voice stops us cold.

"His fault? Now that's jumping to conclusions, isn't it?"

Dr. Allen stands by the open exam door. His face is covered in sweat, and his shirt pocket hangs lopsided, partially ripped off. There are bloodstains on his shirt, and I wonder if it is his blood or Mom's.

Ronan charges at him but stops abruptly as Dr. Allen holds up a long, sharp knife.

"So, you think you figured it out," he snares. "You both disappointment me."

Ronan fumes.

"Why?" I hear myself ask.

The word hangs in the air. I'm not sure why I care, but I do. I want to know why he's doing this. He must have cared about his work and the animals at some point. There must have been something that made my mom invest in a friendship with him. So where did it all go wrong? I realize that I want to understand. I need to understand.

"Because I deserve it. I have always deserved the recognition, but it always went to your father," he spits the words out with such disgust and hatred that fear grips its cold fingers around my heart.

"You were in university together."

"Ah, so you're finally making the connection." He leers at me with disgust swimming in his eyes. "Yeah, we were all in school together. Oliver Foster was loved by all, including your mom—even though I loved her first."

As he moves closer, I notice white fur matted in the blood on his shirt. The spirit bears are here.

"He swooped right in, taking her from me, picking up the best research positions, gaining all the interest of the department chairs. We worked together on the Great Bear Initiative. Did you even know that?" He shoots a challenging look my way, like I'm going to dispute this very fact, and he's waiting for it.

The Great Bear Initiative was the research proposal that brought Dad to Great Bear. He was the lead scientist for as long as I can remember. It was his project. He talked about it all the time. Without that research, our lives would have been so different.

"It was his project," I say defiantly. "He was the lead scientist."

Ronan moves slightly closer to me.

Dr. Allen snorts a half-laugh, half-gag. A glint hits me in the eye, and I recognize his university pin. I've seen him wear it before. I think back to our first night here and the man in the woods. Could it have been Dr. Allen? Maybe he wasn't watching me, but rather Mom.

"Your father and I worked on that proposal together. He never could have done it without me. He was never able to understand the business parts of research. Without that, his proposal was nothing but the scientific hopes and aspirations of a mediocre scientist. It never would have been funded. It wouldn't have the impact it's having now."

"That's why you were in Great Bear last year."

There's pride in his eyes. "You found out about that now, did you?"

His eyes haze over, and it seems like he has traveled back to that day. There's a lack of presence in his look, and Ronan takes the opportunity to slip a scalpel off the exam table and move slightly in front of me.

"Even if what you say is true, my dad was the better scientist because he never would have had anything to do with unethical genetic engineering."

His lips curve into a wicked smile.

"What is ethical research anyway? Is the answer for one man to say?" He gets that far look in his eyes again. "Would you think your dad so ethical if you knew that he never mentioned me or credited my research in his proposal? He was awarded the Great Bear research position, and I was left on my own. My one hope was that your mom would finally realize how good we would be together. I held onto that."

His fists clench in and out in thumping movements. "But that night, we met for coffee like we had planned, and she told me that she was going with your father to Great Bear to be a part of his team. My last hope was gone, and everything I ever wanted was taken from me—by your father."

He looks directly at me. "Is that ethical?"

My mind is overwhelmed with everything he said. Before I can answer, I feel Ronan tense up beside me.

"You look so much like her back then." Dr. Allen takes a few steps closer.

The memory of getting out of his car after homecoming runs through my mind.

"When I first saw you, it was like seeing her the first time we met all those years ago."

His look makes my skin crawl.

Dr. Allen turns to Ronan. "You can still get away. She'll break your heart too. If you come with me, I can promise you more power and wealth than you could ever imagine."

"Never," Ronan growls.

Anger flashes in Dr. Allen's eyes before they land on the scalpel in Ronan's hand. A wicked twist transforms Dr. Allen's mouth into the snarl of a wild animal. I can feel his control breaking. I need to stop him.

"Where are the spirit bears?" My question throws him for a moment, but the sinister grin returns. "They're here. I know it."

"You and McFadden were in on it together, weren't you?" Ronan says, barely controlling his anger.

He rolls his eyes in an exasperated shake of his head. "That idiot, McFadden. He was a good vet; I'll give him that. But he couldn't do anything else right. Then he got caught like a petty thief. I should have known that if I wanted something done right, I'd have to do it myself. I went to Great Bear to wipe away any of the evidence that he was stupid enough to leave."

He didn't clean everything up though. The ring was still there.

"It was then that I decided to camp out for a bit and go for the cub. It was supposed to be my reward and the start of our research."

"You killed my dad." My heartbeat thunders in my head, making it hard to understand.

Something like sadness flashes over his face. "I didn't want to. I was so close to the cub, but your dad got between us and—"

"He recognized you." Ronan grips the scalpel tighter, his knuckles turning white.

"I couldn't let him win again."

"Is that why you asked Mom to take the vet position here? So, you could finally win?"

His eyes seem to plead with me to be on his side. "I love your mom. I always have. But she was also a threat to the operation. I needed you both out of Great Bear. It was a mistake to bring you here.

That was my fault because I wanted to be with her so badly. When the questions started and you took it upon yourselves to play detectives, that is when we knew you had to go."

"So you sent the notes?" Ronan asks.

His smile is lethal. "Actually, no." I can see he's enjoying letting us in on this secret. "Who do you know that always has plenty of stationary around?"

No, it can't be. "Ms. Maggie," I whisper.

"You got another one right!" He snickers at his own joke. "Good ol' Ms. Maggie. She's always a good player. Her grandson was my protégé during my graduate days at Berkeley. He looked up to me, and Ms. Maggie welcomed me into their family. It was with his encouragement that I created the Fraternity of Valor, a place where I could finally get the respect I deserved for so long."

"Nathan." I can barely get out his name. Nathan is her grandson.

Sirens sound in the distance. Help is on the way.

Ronan glares at him. "You're not going to pull this off. We know it's you, and so do the police. You're going to have to pay for everything that you've done."

"You've always been a good boy."

Ronan flinches at the familiar female voice.

Ms. Maggie is standing in the doorway, dressed in her ranger outfit with a camouflage bandana wrapped around her head. Frazzled white hair sticks out like thorns on a rose bush. Her eyes are widely exhilarated, giving her that frenzied appearance I remember the from the first day I met her.

"What? Good ol' Ms. Maggie surprised y'all good this time, didn't I? Tada!" She swings her hands around in the space before her in an exaggerated bow, a black handgun swinging in her hand.

"Oh, don't look so hurt." She looks at Ronan and sighs, like she's telling a little child he can't have more chocolate. "I tried to keep you and Colin out of this, but you two are always playing hero. I even tried to keep pretty Dr. Foster safe, but she couldn't leave this alone either."

All eyes go to Mom on the floor. Instinctively I bend down, placing my hand on her forehead. A soft groan escapes her mouth, and she turns her head slightly. I steal a glance at Dr. Allen, and he's looking at her as if for the first time, the color seeping from his face. All the frantic energy he had only moments ago drains, leaving him limp and lifeless. Is it possible he hadn't seen her there?

"That wasn't part of the plan. She wasn't to be harmed." His voice is genuine, filled with confusion and denial, the workings of a lunatic finally starting to see the reality of the situation.

I realize in this moment how much he really loves Mom. He never wanted her to get hurt, and somehow in his crazed state, he hadn't noticed her on the floor. Something has changed in him now. He doesn't look like the same man he was a couple minutes ago.

The sirens are louder now.

It's only a matter of time, but I don't see how this can end well.

"Now, Eric," Ms. Maggie commands. "It's time."

She points at me. "She's all yours. This is what you have been working so hard for." She coaxes Dr. Allen, sounding like a mother who soothes her child and leads him to where she wants him to go.

Dr. Allen looks at me, perplexed by what to say.

"Now!" Ms. Maggie's voice echoes in the small room. But she's not looking at me anymore. She glares at Dr. Allen.

The sirens are right outside now. Car doors slam, and a man's voice barks orders.

"I won't let you hurt her again," Dr. Allen mumbles, swaying slightly on his feet. He stares directly at Ms. Maggie.

Ronan steps between me and Ms. Maggie, his scalpel a David to Ms. Maggie's Goliath.

An old verse from the Bible runs through my mind—"No one has greater love than this, to lay down one's life for one's friends."

"Always the hero," she shakes her head at Ronan.

The door to the clinic crashes down, and in the flash of movement, two gunshots ring out, leaving a deafening silence.

And then everything goes dark.

SMOKE SINGES MY NOSTRILS, awakening me to the smoky night sky. Something hard is rubbing against my upper lip. My fingers trace a plastic tubing. Pulling it away, I see it's connected to oxygen on a stretcher. I try to bolt upright, but the belts strain my stomach and legs. There's a dull pounding in my head, threatening to get worse, like the feeling just before a migraine begins.

People are rushing around. Luckily, no one seems to notice me as I unhook the safety belts. The EMTs are wheeling another stretcher to an ambulance, with a white sheet pulled over the body.

Someone's dead.

My heart gallops like a thousand horses. Mom? Ronan?

I try to shake the fog from my brain. I recall the gunshots—so loud that they shook the exam table, and glassware clattered to the floor. Then a heavy weight fell on me, and everything went black. I touch my head where the throbbing worsens and feel the wet gauze, blood staining my fingers.

"We need an ETA on the planes. The fire is growing," a deep voice crackles on a radio from a makeshift command base. A police officer answers, "Three to five minutes."

A fire burns wildly in the sanctuary. My thundering heart seems now to have stopped completely.

I need to do something.

Glancing around to make sure no one is looking, I slide off the stretcher, unhooking the IV-fluid line. I cut behind the clinic and around to the side of the sanctuary. Flames are leaping as if in a synchronized dance. The path to the stables has been roped off. The fire deadly spreads close to it now. The whinnying of the horses pierces the air. Without hesitation, I shimmy down the edge of the rope, staying in the shadows and run toward the stable.

Sweat flows down my face, leaving trails in the soot. I stop to tear a strip of satin fabric from the bottom of my dress and throw my shoes to the side. I cover my mouth with the soft fabric, hoping to block some of the smoke. Someone yells my name, but I don't turn around. Instead, I run straight ahead into the path of the blaze until I'm gasping for air.

The pounding of hooves against wood sounds frantic as the horses are getting desperate to escape. I slide the front door, quickly closing it behind me to deter the fire as long as possible. I slide open the back door, and the horses sound manic to escape. I run down the aisle, unlatching the stalls. Each horse takes off into the night. Cosmo pauses by me, his blue eyes reflecting the flames that now consume the stable, before running after the other horses, in search of safe ground.

My adrenaline subsides, and I fall over coughing. Everything is too hot. The flames are too close. My head pounds, and my throat is parched, like rough, scorching sand. Everything begins spinning, and I don't know what direction I'm going in or what path to take. I take a step but sway back and forth, unable to maintain my balance or direction. I'm lost in the sea of fire, threatening to swallow me whole.

The swirling flames tease and taunt me, beckoning me closer and closer until images of the past form memories in its fiery tendrils. I see myself laughing, young and carefree. Running through the rainforest, I glance behind to see my parents chasing close behind. Dad catches me and swings me around in a circle as Mom laughs by his side. My stomach knots at the memory, but the flame almost immediately swirls, and the image is lost in the night.

The fire is even hotter now, oozing like a river of blood. Scorching flames singe my dress, attempting to pull me in as smoke fills my lungs. I can't breathe. I feel myself drifting away, and I can no longer hold on as I fall to the ground. The heat pierces my skin like needles, but I don't move. Everything looks hazy, and I close my eyes, letting the darkness come.

Angel stands in front of me, gentleness in her expression. From behind her is something greater, a translucent glow, radiating peace. The warmth fills my soul. The light leads Angel to me. She bends low, and I wrap my arms around her neck. I feel myself lifting off the ground, my legs once again able to hold my weight, and I walk with the light guiding me. The heat seems to have receded, and all I feel is her soft fur as she guides me out of the stable. The light casts a protective glow behind us. We make it about fifteen feet, before the stable comes crashing down, sparks shooting into the dark sky. Screams ring through the air.

My eyes shoot open, and I cough up phlegm. As I stand outside the stable, the fresh air refreshes my lungs. The glimmer from the translucent light remains, and I feel the uncontrollable urge to go to it. As I get closer, my entire body fills with a merciful love. Guilt and doubt break like chains from my heart, and I feel free. Renewed with strength and determination, I vow to do everything I can to make things right. Inhaling fresh air back into my lungs, I run as fast as I can back to the clinic.

I am not going to let this be the end of the story.

———

WHEN I REACH THE CLINIC, Ronan is yelling at the fire chief while a medic grips his arm. The moment he sees me, he runs and wraps me in a hug. One of his shirt sleeves is cut to just below the shoulder, and a large white bandage wraps around his upper arm, blood staining the center. His face is cut and swollen on the right side.

"Thank God you're okay." He kisses the top of my head.

"Your arm." I gently touch the bandage.

"A bullet. But it only grazed me."

I hug him tighter as our reality comes back, hitting me like a ton of bricks. "My mom?"

"She's okay. She has a concussion, but she's going to be just fine. They took her to Redwood Hills Hospital. She looked much better when they left—awake and asking for you."

Relief washes over me.

It's then that I see Ms. Maggie. She's handcuffed, sitting in the back of the sheriff's car, looking right at me. Her red lips curl in a cruel snare. I don't look away though, staring right back at her until she finally looks away with a roll of her eyes. A few officers are standing around the car talking to a woman who looks like—

"Ms. Hannon?"

She's dressed in jeans and a white button-down shirt. A badge is clipped to her belt as well as a handgun. Her weight shifts to one leg as she takes notes on a legal pad.

"Yeah, so apparently, she's an undercover FBI agent. She came here to investigate the poaching ring, working undercover as a teacher. The FBI got wind of the potential research, and she's been following Dr. Allen and Ms. Maggie for months now."

"What happened?" I whisper. "Everything went dark after the gunshots."

Ronan's face scrunches in pain. "When Ms. Maggie fired the shots, one hit my arm, and the other got Dr. Allen. Sadie, he jumped on you and your mom. If he hadn't—"

His body was the weight I felt. I must have bumped my head when he fell on us.

"Where is he?"

Ronan doesn't say anything, but I see the answer in his eyes. That was the body I saw on the stretcher. He gave up his life for us.

It's hard to see Dr. Allen as any kind of hero. I mean, he was horrible. He killed Dad. He's been stealing the spirit bears and planning on using them for illegal genetic research. He was full of hate. As soon as I reflect on it, I know the truth. He was drowning in resentment, but he loved Mom. In the end that love was stronger than everything else. His love was so deep that he gave his life to save me, so to not cause her more pain.

I rest my head against Ronan's chest and look up into his eyes to see that he has reached the same conclusion. Sighing deeply, I carefully touch the side of his face. "What happened to your face?"

"Colin."

"Ranger Anderson?" My shock makes him laugh.

"When I saw you running into the fire, I yelled and tried to go after you, but Colin stopped me. But not without a fight, as you can see."

Ronan was the one I heard calling my name. I shake my head at his sheepish expression and trace his budding bruises with my finger. "When are you going to learn that I can take care of myself?"

"When you learn that I'll never stop trying to protect you."

For a moment all the noise fades, and it's only the two of us. I want more answers, but the time will come. Right now, the only place I want to be is in his arms.

CHAPTER SIXTEEN

It could have been a lot worse. We will rebuild, and it will be even better than before. The remains of the stable are piled up before me. Scooping up a handful of ashes, I let them slide through my fingers to the ground. In darkness there is always light. In despair there is hope. From the ash will come new life.

The ring rests in my hand. The cold metal is hard against my skin. I look at the symbol. Spirit. Dr. Allen was so obsessed with being the most powerful and having it all that he allowed it to take over his life. Always desiring more and more, he became filled with greed and the lust for power. He lost his family, his profession, and his dreams. Everything became distorted in greed and revenge. My heart hurts for a life lost and all the damage it caused in our community here and in Great Bear.

The entire town was shocked to learn about Ms. Maggie's involvement in the poaching ring and illegal research. She was not the woman we all thought she was. She's in jail now, awaiting her trial. But, even after everything, I hope that she will change during her time there.

That's what I've learned from this past year. No matter what happens or how bad things become, there's always hope. The guilt I felt for so long had crushed me in its grip. I couldn't move on until I broke away from its hold. Only now can I begin to forgive others.

Nathan has disappeared. I don't doubt that he will still be around, always watching and lurking in the background and showing up when we least expect it. He wasn't the mastermind of this operation, but he was the one who added to the fire of Dr. Allen's resentment and anger. His grandmother, wrapped around his finger, would do anything to make him happy. They are a dangerous pair, and they played everyone, including Dr. Allen.

The FBI hasn't been able to locate any of the research documents. They searched the Fraternity's headquarters in San Francisco, questioning all the known members, but they've hit a dead-end. We don't know the goal of their research, but I have a feeling it's not the last we're going to hear of it. The documents and samples have all vanished without a trace, locked and hidden somewhere, just waiting to be reopened. Knowing that they're still out there leaves me with a cold anticipation of what might come next. But no matter what happens, I know that I am not alone.

———

THE SPIRIT BEARS are discovered a few days later at an enclosure not far from where Rocky and I ran into that mountain lion. It's the reason Dr. Allen was there that day. I noticed at the time how suspicious Ranger Anderson looked of him being there, but it wasn't until after the fire that I learned that he and Ms. Hannon had been in touch throughout the whole investigation. I thought the two men just didn't get along, but now I know that he had grounds not to trust him. This came as another shock to Ronan, but the two have never been closer.

Standing at the enclosure, I take in the spirit bears' appearance, looking so out of place. They all survived the ordeal, and plans are already in the works for transport back to Great Bear. Anna and the team are thrilled we are safe, and the bears are coming home. I snap a picture of the bears and send it to her. That pull of homesickness comes but abates quickly. In a way, Great Bear will always be my home.

It doesn't take away from the love I have for Redwood Hills or the home we've made here.

"They're incredible," Ronan says with that same awe so many of the visitors at Great Bear have the first time they visit. It dawns on me that while he's seen pictures and heard everything about them, this is his first time seeing the spirit bears. That experience is one never to be forgotten. While I know that everyone thinks this is my moment to reunite with Angel, I realize it's also his.

"It's like seeing the northern lights for the first time," I whisper to him.

His smile widens at the memory. "Yeah, it sure is, and I don't have my camera this time either."

"Yes, you do," Ranger Anderson says from behind us, handing Ronan his camera.

"You think this makes up for everything?" Ronan snaps back.

"I already told you—I couldn't tell you. It could have messed up the investigation. What should I have done?"

Their banter warms my heart.

"Are you feeling okay?"

She glides her fingers over the bandage on her head. "Yes, I'm feeling much better. Colin is making sure I'm well taken care of." She smiles at Ranger Anderson. "How are you doing, sweetheart?"

Just a few days ago that would have been a loaded question, but today there's only one answer. "I'm hopeful."

Mom slides an arm around my shoulders, pulling me in for a warm hug.

"I haven't had any more dreams about Angel, but I'm not scared of them anymore. There was so much darkness, but now I've realized that every dream had a light in the darkness."

Mom nods. "The light is the way out of darkness."

"For me, it was working through Angel. I just wish it hadn't taken me so long to see it."

"Look," Ronan says, pointing to the far side of the enclosure. "Here she comes."

We watch as Angel walks through the group and straight toward us. She's weak and has cuts and scrapes on her body. Her ragged bones jerk under her skin, and I wish I could heal her and promise her that nothing bad will ever happen to her again. But I know I can't.

Her cub is up on his hind legs looking quizzically between me and his mom. His creamy, downy fur sticks up in matted sections. Angel rolls to her side, allowing the cub to nurse.

"Thank you," I whisper, "for helping me to see the truth."

THE RESEARCH TEAM drives over to the diner together after one of the longest and most emotional days of my life. Even with all the normal noise and commotion, the place seems empty without Gia.

When we left the after-prom party, Gia ended up telling her sister about everything. Worried that our suspicions were right, they got Evan and followed us to the clinic. They reached it just after the police had arrived and saw the clinic in its crime-scene state.

Evan has been with Gia the whole time, sending updates to me and Ronan. He says that her whole family is in shock, but Gia was doing okay. Her parents are flying in tomorrow to be with them. Her mother is beyond herself with worry, saying Gia needs to come home. We're hoping it's the emotions talking right now, and Gia will be allowed to stay. But with everything that has happened, it's hard to know what to expect in the coming days.

I guess only time will tell what will happen to us all.

THE BELL RINGS for the last time, and chairs scrape the floor as loud voices drift out into the hallway. I watch as students rush out of the classroom, calling to friends all excited for summer break to begin. Redwood Academy does a reverse-schedule day on the last day of school, so today biology is my last class. One of the guys on the baseball team challenges Ronan to a race down the hallway, which he gladly accepts while I just shake my head. Is this what the end of the school year is like every year? While the excitement is contagious, I know that I'll miss being here. It's been five weeks since the night of the fire, and the end of the school year brings with it both sadness and excitement.

Gia's parents left last week. They spent the past month mourning the loss of Dr. Allen and deciding what will happen with Gia. After much convincing, her parents have agreed to allow Gia to stay. This was a huge relief to everyone, and the whole experience seems to have brought Gia and her sister even closer than they were before. It's like even during so much tragedy, there's always good that shines through.

That good continues tomorrow as Ronan, Gia, Evan, and I are traveling with the research team to return the spirit bears to Great Bear. The two teams have been communicating back and forth, and we are now all set to transport them back home. Looks like my two worlds will be coming together again, and I can't wait.

As I get up from my desk, looking out the window one last time, Mrs. Buonaparte calls to me from the doorway.

"I heard you're taking the advanced design course this summer. So I guess I'll be seeing you around here."

"Yes," I gush with the same pride and excitement I felt when Ms. Auclair first told me that I was selected to be part of the summer art program. "I'm so excited."

Just like that, I'm reminded that the most important things aren't necessarily the ones we have planned for but the opportunities that arise each and every day.

Ronan shows up at the door, looking sweaty and out of breath. "You two have a nice summer and try to stay out of trouble." She winks at us as she walks away.

I hadn't known what to expect when I came to Redwood Hills, but I know that finding my place here was not what I ever imagined it would be. Looking at my life now, I can't imagine not being here with Ronan or hanging out with Gia and Evan every day.

As Ronan and I walk through the hallway, memories from this year fly through my mind. Some are so amazing that I hope I will always remember them as clearly as I do today. Others are so sad that my heart aches with just the thought. The bright sun shines on us as we leave the building in what feels like a momentous gesture.

"Took you two long enough," Evan yells to us from his Jeep. "Seriously, the last day of school, and we're the last people here. Something's wrong with that."

"Something's wrong with you," Gia retorts, sitting next to him in the front seat and fixing her ponytail in the rearview mirror. Evan rustles her hair, and she punches him on the arm.

We climb into his Jeep as "School's Out" blares from the radio.

I wipe my eye as a runaway tear escapes. "What's wrong?" Ronan asks.

"Nothing. Everything's just so, so right."

"THAT'S NOT A CURVEBALL," Evan yells. "I'll show you a real curveball."

Evan, Ronan, and Jason play a friendly game of catch, or at least we thought it was a friendly game. Apparently, Evan thinks they're training for the next World Series.

"Not bad," Anna calls, "but I think I'd better come down there and show you how it's really done."

Anna jogs down and throws what could only be considered the best throw of their game, leaving Evan speechless for once.

"Okay, she is awesome." Gia pulls her hair up into a messy bun.

I'm so happy that Gia and Anna seem to be off to a much better start this time around. But I wonder if Jason has something to do with that. Gia hit it off with Jason from the moment we arrived in Great Bear two days ago.

It has been so nice catching up with everyone again. The mood is festive, distinctly different than it was over Christmas break. Laughter fills the air, and stories are being shared back and forth like everyone has known each other forever. The two research teams have made quite the connection, and I think there will be more joint research happening in the future.

The night of the fire has become like a legend at the base. Everyone is talking about it and thanking us for our part in the rescue. Evan said he feels like a celebrity, which, of course, he absolutely loves. Mama Rose is delighted with the sketches I've showed her for the bed quilt I'm planning for my summer design course.

The spirit bears handled the trip well, and they are quickly adjusting back to the rainforest. Most of the hair on their necks has grown back in from where the collars were, wiping away the last of the physical reminders of what happened. Papa Jay has promised to watch them closely to make sure their emotional scars are healing as well.

"Dinner is ready!" Mama Rose's voice rings out, calling us back up to the deck. The smell of grilled barbecue salmon drifts through the air, and my stomach grumbles in anticipation.

My phone vibrates with a new text message.

"We're all missing you so much. Give everyone our love."

It's a photo of Mom and Ranger Anderson with Angel and her cub. The two bears are still too weak to make the journey home. Mom and Colin have them in a special enclosure at the sanctuary where they can continue to recover and receive the best care until they're healthy enough to return to Great Bear. They are getting better every day, and we hope to have them back home soon. I have to admit that I enjoy having them at the sanctuary though. When I take Cosmo out for a trail ride, we often go by their enclosure, and it warms my heart seeing them there—a piece of Great Bear in Redwood Hills.

I know it will be hard to part from them when the time comes, but I am going to take life one step at a time. I don't want to look too far ahead, and I'm finished looking back. The past is the past for a reason. You learn from it, but you don't live it again and again. I spent so much time reliving my past that I couldn't embrace the present, and I don't want to fall into that trap again.

After dinner, Papa Jay nods, and I know it's time. I reach into the pocket of my long, yellow cotton dress, the material softly wrapping around my hand, until I feel the familiar metal. We all walk to the river together, to the place where everything changed. I walk with confidence and the understanding that there was meaning in this tragedy. There was purpose to this suffering. That day was not the end, only the next step in a long journey.

When we get to the spot, I see the stone marker Papa Jay and the team carved for Dad—a hero's tribute. I take the wildflowers I picked from the forest and place them next to the stone.

"I love you, Dad."

We can let the past darkness overwhelm us, or we can choose to allow the light to shine through the darkness. I choose the light.

I feel the peace that my soul has longed for. I know that no matter how dark things become, even the smallest spark of hope can be enough to chase away the darkness.

Whatever may come, I'm ready for it.

AUTHOR'S NOTE

I remember standing among the towering redwood trees of northern California and being in awe of their majestic size and quiet strength. It's in moments like those where the beauty of God's creation fills my heart and leaves a lasting impression. When I began drafting *Sadie's Star* I felt drawn to the redwoods and the nearby Great Bear Rainforest. The story evolved to include two of the most incredible ecosystems in the world.

The Redwood National Park provides a welcome home to black bears, mountain lions, Roosevelt elk, gray whales, the banana slug, bald eagles, and many other plants and animals. Park staff work to maintain and restore the area's biological diversity on a daily basis. They strive to preserve both the natural processes and the region's species and genetic diversity to ensure that countless generations will be able to experience this wonderous place.

The Great Bear Rainforest is a treasure found along the northern and central coast of British Columbia. It is a temperate rain forest comprising of more than 250 miles of forest and costal land. The land provides for 1,000-year-old cedars, moss-covered mountains, glacier-cut fjords, and hundreds of waterfalls and streams. Great Bear is home to abundant wildlife such as coastal gray wolves, cougars, Sitka deer, grizzly bears, sea otters, mountain goats, orca, sea lions, and the rare cream-colored Kermode bear, or commonly called the spirit bear. The Great Bear Rainforest is protected by the indigenous people of the region and the Great Bear Rainforest Education and Trust.

To learn more about the Redwood National Park and the Great Bear Rainforest, visit https://www.nps.gov/redw/planyourvisit/basicin fo.htm and https://greatbearrainforesttrust.org

ACKNOWLEDGMENTS

I want to start as always by thanking you, the reader, for joining Sadie on her journey. I hope you enjoyed your time in Redwood Hill and Great Bear. I invite you to join my newsletter to learn about upcoming releases and giveaways.

Wishing heartfelt thanks to:

All of my early readers. Your feedback, reviews, and testimonials mean so much.

To my SNHU MFA professors, especially Professor Hart. Thank you for believing in me and this story.

My editor, Jody Benson, for helping refine this story. Your support is greatly appreciated.

Hannah Linder Designs for creating the perfect cover for *Sadie's Star*.

All those who strive every day to protect the natural beauty of God's creation.

Grandma Sadie, for whom this book is named.

My family and friends for your unceasing support. Especially, my parents for your constant love and life-giving experiences.

Connor, Brody, and Emma for inspiring me every day. I love you so much!

My husband, Bill, to whom this book is dedicated. I love you and I am so grateful to live this life with you.

And above all else, to Jesus to planting the dream of writing and a love of nature in my heart. I strive to share Your love in my words.

MEET THE AUTHOR

Colleen Marie grew up writing stories and dreaming of one day sharing them with the world. She earned her MFA in Creative Writing and is a member of the Catholic Writers Guild and American Christian Fiction Writers. A great love of animals and teaching led her to a career as a life scientist and science educator. Animals weave their way into her tales, bringing a sense of the natural world with the fictional. Her stories inspire readers to see the natural beauty in God's creation.

Colleen Marie lives in a small town in northern Maryland with her husband, three children, and crew of lovable animal friends. When she's not writing, you can find her teaching biology at a local university, enjoying family hikes through the woods, and traveling to find the most amazing homemade ice cream.

Visit her website at www.onespiritoflove.com and sign up for her monthly newsletter to learn about new releases, giveaways, and personal stories! Follow along with her adventures on social media @onespiritoflove.

OTHER BOOKS BY COLLEEN MARIE

Teagan's Treasure
New Adult Fiction Novel
Emerald Isle University Series Book #1
Paperback ISBN: 979-8-9880122-8-3

Teagan O'Reilly has one goal upon graduation – to be accepted into Emerald Isle University's Science Research Internship and spend the summer in Ireland competing for a spot in the university's coveted research program. When her acceptance letter finally arrives, Teagan is more determined than ever to win a spot into the program. She's prepared for everything until she learns her partner is none other than Finn Connolly, her first love and the boy who broke her heart.

Past feelings reignite as Teagan and Finn travel to Brigid's Crossing in the small town of Cloverdale, Ireland, to begin their internship. Their research project quickly comes to life on the Kavanagh's horse farm, bringing new life to the farm and Teagan's dreams.

Teagan soon discovers that the farm is in financial trouble, jeopardizing her meticulously planned research, and it needs a miracle to be saved. The rolling hills of the Irish countryside are hiding a secret, and the answer may lie in the legendary tale of the missing Kildare Emerald. When a plot to steal the emerald from the Kavanagh's land is uncovered, the safety of farm and their chance at the research position lies in the balance.

As time begins to run out, Teagan is torn between winning the research position and helping the Kavanagh's save the farm. Teagan is forced to decide where her heart lies, but will her choice make her lose everything she's always dreamed of, or will she gain more than she ever imagined?

9 798218 502591